I0619879

If He Comes Back

Kate Browning

To request permission, please contact:
MJCMediaPA@gmail.com

ISBN: 979-8988441526

Names, characters, places and events are products of the author's imagination. Any similarity to real persons, living or dead is coincidental and not intended by the author or publisher.

Table of Contents

If He Comes Back

ONE

Isabella Rossi, Izzy to those who knew her well, sat in her favorite chair, feet up on the ottoman, the soft crackle of the fireplace seemed to be in sync with the soft pitter-patter of rain against the window. Wrapping her fingers around a steaming mug of coffee, she let the warmth seep into her skin, into her bones, chasing away the chill of the autumn night. But the heat from the coffee couldn't relieve the aching she felt in her chest. It was on nights like these that it would come back to her. No matter how she tried to suppress it, it remained.

Three years had passed since Ethan left Willow's End. He wanted more than this tiny seaside town could offer. Being an architect in this environment wasn't going to work, and he didn't want to be anything else. There was no job here that would make him happy. He could only realize his dreams if he moved closer to where his skills were needed. That meant moving closer to a large city. Something Izzy didn't want to do.

He'd kissed her goodbye under the glow of her porch light. It was the same spot where he had once promised her they'd be together forever. But forever turned out to be very fragile, easily broken by the drive of ambition. Ethan had chosen to pursue his creative aspirations in the city, far from the tranquility of their little town.

She had often second-guessed her decision not to go with him. He had asked, but she couldn't leave her beloved home or the life she had begun to build here. She had no desire to trade the peace and beauty of Willow's End for the chaos and noise of a big city. Izzy knew she had to let Ethan go.

It hadn't been easy, but she knew if he stayed he would not be happy. He would always wonder what he could have achieved. Eventually, he would have resented not going after his dreams. More than anything, Izzy couldn't handle the thought that someday he might resent her, too, for being the reason he stayed. So, with tears in her eyes and a shattered heart, she let him go.

Though he didn't occupy her thoughts several times a day, as he once had, Izzy still found herself missing his company. Especially on nights like this, with the fire burning and the rain against the window, she wished Ethan was sitting in the chair next to her. She would close her eyes and envision it, holding hands, drinking coffee and having the kind of easy conversation they used to have that was always sprinkled with laughter. She could see the firelight reflected in his eyes and the confident grin that would always melt her heart. The lonliness would subside during those moments, only to return again once she opened her eyes.

Izzy learned to fill the void by keeping herself busy—her bookstore that smelled of paper and promise, and the comforting embrace of her friends and community. She found hobbies that interested her, including painting. Learning to paint was something she had wanted to do since she was in high school, but between opening her store and Ethan, she put it aside. Now, she would often take her easel down to the beach near the pier and paint the ocean at various angles and at different times of the day. But what brought her the most comfort was going inland to Winding Lake. It was there among the willows, quiet and serene, that she found the most inspiration.

And she got herself a dog, a husky she named Jasper. Her friends had told her to get a cat, but she thought that was too cliché. She spotted Jasper online and immediately fell in love. She drove nearly three hours to pick him up from the owners who were moving and couldn't take him with them. He was only two when she got him. Now, at five, he still acted like an energetic puppy. He kept her on her toes, snuggled on the bed with her at night, and was her walking, painting and watching TV partner. Wherever Izzy was, Jasper wasn't too far behind.

She did date a bit since Ethan left, however, no one sparked her interest. Though she knew, in her soul, she really wasn't giving any of them a real chance, though she could not explain why. She thought, maybe, it was because she still thought of Ethan, but the truth was it usually only came down to times like this; a cool autumn night, snuggled with a fire, that he would come back to her thoughts.

Izzy could have gone with him or she could have convinced him to stay. They could have built a life together. At the end of the day, when she returned to the solitude of her home, she was met with the echoes of what once was and thoughts of what could have been if he had stayed or she had gone. Yet, she knew it would not have worked. She would have been miserable in a city and he would not have been happy staying.

Her best friend, Claire, often pushed her to get out more. Claire had even convinced her to try a few dating apps. Izzy tried half-heartedly. Most of them were divorced men and she took that as a red flag. Her parents had left

Willow's End after retiring, her first real love, Brian, had left after graduating college. She still thought about Brian fairly often but he'd gotten a job, gotten married and never came back. And then Ethan had left. Not to mention a handful of other friends who had taken off after high school. Izzy didn't need another person leaving and a divorce signaled an established record of leaving. Claire disagreed with that assessment, but it's what Izzy felt. Jasper was the only male she wanted to have around long-term.

These nights, though, by the fire. These were the nights she missed having someone there and Ethan was there in her thoughts. She would reminisce about the bike rides they would take with the fall colors as a beautiful backdrop, or the hikes through the forest, leaves crunching under their feet.

Tonight, as she sipped her coffee and listened to the fire, Jasper's head in her lap, she began to wonder if she would find someone to fill the hole inside. The hole made bigger each time someone she loved left. She shook her head and chuckled to herself. She was enjoying the life she had built for herself, she had good friends and her parents were only a phone call away. *Why do I want a man?* she thought. *They only complicate things*. She gave Jasper's ears a rub and turned her attention back to the fire.

The ding of her phone interrupted her thoughts. She picked it up from her side table and saw a text from Claire.

Open the front door. I'll be over in 10.
Get out the wine glasses.

Izzy chuckled softly. Claire knew her so well it was almost frightening. Claire knew she'd be sitting here, feeling a bit lonely with a few thoughts of an ex-boyfriend going through her mind. She loved Claire, but she was tired and not up for the company. She clicked out her response.

Thanks, girl, but I'm done for the night.
Appreciate it, though!

She set the phone on her lap, knowing there would be a response coming. Jasper jumped down, made his way to his bed by the fireplace, took a look back at Izzy and then made himself comfortable. The phone dinged again.

Nope. Got a surprise for you.

Claire, seriously, I'm tired.
Another night?

Nope. We're coming.
Get out three glasses.

Who's the third?

You'll see. Trust me, you'll be surprised.
Just make sure the front door is open.

I'm intrigued.

See you soon!

Glad she hadn't changed out of her clothes or taken her makeup off after work, Izzy got off her chair and headed to the kitchen. Jasper was right behind her. She bent down and scratched his ears, talking to him like she always did, telling him they were getting company and he should be on his best behavior.

She hadn't lied to Claire. She was tired, but she was also intrigued as to who she was bringing with her and why it had been labeled a surprise. After taking down three wine glasses and checking herself in the mirror, Izzy returned to her chair and checked her phone. She scrolled through a few apps and was about to check her email when she heard a car door slam shut, followed closely by another. Jasper was already up and howling by the door.

Shooing Jasper from the door and commanding him to sit, Izzy opened the door and greeted Claire.

"Hey, you!" Claire smiled broadly and wrapped her arms around Izzy, wine bottle in hand.

Looking over her friend's shoulder, Izzy couldn't easily identify the man who was standing a few feet behind Claire, though there was something very familiar about him. He was turned, looking back at her front yard. For a moment split second she thought she knew, and her heart skipped a beat, but realized it was would be impossible. She took a step back from Claire and smiled. Claire handed her the bottle of wine and stepped into the house.

"Are you coming in?" Claire asked playfully, looking back toward the door and then smiled knowingly at Izzy.

The man turned and Izzy froze. She'd been right. It was him. His features had grown and changed over the years, but it was definitely him. The hair, the eyes, the smile, she knew them in an instant, but her mind refused to believe he was standing on her porch. She knew her mouth had dropped open but she seemed unable to move or to form any clear thought.

"I knew you'd be surprised!" Claire exclaimed. "I ran into him at the post office this afternoon. I couldn't believe it."

"Hey, Izzy, it's been a while." The voice was as deep as she remembered it.

Shaking herself from the shock, she gushed, "Brian! What are you doing here?" Without another thought, she rushed to embrace him.

"Oh my God! I can't believe this," Izzy continued as she backed up. "I never thought you'd be back here. Maybe for the 25th or 50th class reunion, but certainly not now. Come in! Tell me what brought you back."

"Long story," he replied as he entered the house. "Let's open the wine and I'll tell you about it."

Izzy shut the door and, later, as Brian was telling them a short version of why he came back to Willow's End, she could hardly believe he was standing there. The boy who had taken her to the prom, the boy who she had her high school years with, had grown into a handsome, well-built man. He had been her first love, and the boy she had lost her virginity to one moonlit, magical night out at Winding Lake.

As she took in the greenish-gray eyes, the dark hair and the strong arms, several memories of those long-ago days came back to her. They filled her with a sort of happy nostalgia. Brian was talking about how he'd only gotten back to town the day before, but she barely heard him. Looking at him brought a feeling back to her that she wasn't expecting.

She was taken aback by the feeling, and even more so when she realized her heart had skipped a few beats and there were butterflies in her stomach.

In that moment, Izzy realized that despite the passage of time she was still very much attracted to him. The realization that Brian had triggered a feeling - a very familiar one, yet one she hadn't felt in years gave her a very uneasy feeling. She admonished herself, he was married and off limits.

"Tomorrow we're gonna go through some things, finish packing up the house and then my Dad'll move up north with Doug," Brian was saying as Izzy refocused on the conversation.

"I knew it was rough on him after your mother passed," Claire said, "but I didn't realize he was feeling so lonely. It's been a couple of years. After a while, he seemed like his usual self again whenever we saw him. He was down at the Veteran's Club pretty often. We thought he was doing alright. We should have checked in on him more, visited more."

"I'm sorry, Brian," Izzy added. "I got caught up in too many things going on. That's no excuse. I should have made the time to go see him more. The last time I was there it seemed as if he was doing well. Again, no excuse."

Brian shook his head, "Don't start feeling guilty. Either of you. Dad's very good at pretending everything is fine. He didn't want anyone feeling sorry for him. Even when he had his heart surgery he didn't want people fussing over him." He turned toward Izzy. "You remember that; how difficult he was."

Izzy let out a soft laugh. "I remember. Your mom was so frustrated with him. I remember your brother threatening to strap him down."

"Yeah," Brian chuckled. "He always had a soft spot for you, though. Whenever you asked him to sit down or go rest, he would do that fake grumble but he'd do it." Brian looked up and caught her eyes.

It might have been her imagination, but as Brian looked at her, she felt a stirring, a feeling as if no time had passed. She felt like they could pick up right where they had left off ten years earlier – if he wasn't married. She was fairly certain Brian felt the same. At least that was what she thought she saw in his eyes before he turned his gaze back to Claire and picked up the conversation again.

"Doug got most of the stuff packed up, except for Mom's things. Dad wants us to go through them tomorrow. I guess he thinks there might be things we'll want."

"Of course, there will be," Izzy said. "She kept everything. . .and I do mean everything. I remember the big scrapbooks she put together. She cut out every little article in the paper if your name was mentioned and during baseball season it was mentioned a lot. She was your biggest fan."

Claire laughed. "I remember her cheering you on at the games, especially pee-wee baseball."

The three of them started laughing and in unison, Claire and Izzy started chanting, "Go, baby! Go, baby! Go, baby! Bri!" They followed it with exuberant clapping.

Claire looked over at Brian, "You were Baby Bri until the 10th grade."

"Ninth," Brian corrected, then looked down with a half-smile, clearly reminiscing.

For a moment Izzy saw the young boy he used to be in that smile. She remembered those days. All of them. Claire's father coached the younger teams. They would go down to the park and wait for the games to be over so they could talk him into taking them for ice cream.

Izzy watched the games and, naturally, heard Brian's mom cheer him on at each one. She wasn't particularly interested in any of the boys until middle school. It was the summer before 8th grade when she developed a crush on Brian. He didn't seem to notice her, though. She would linger a little longer after the games, but he'd talk to her like he always did and then he'd take off with his friends after giving his mom a quick hug.

It was another player, Jason, who'd taken an interest in her. She liked Jason, but not as much as she liked Brian. Being young and since Brian showed no interest, she accepted when Jason asked her to go to the movies. For a few weeks that summer, she would go to the games and then walk hand-in-hand with Jason to get ice cream, they'd hang out at the park or go down to Pizza Palace. Her first kiss was with Jason as they sat on the monkey bars on a summer afternoon. She thought it was a good kiss even though she had no basis for comparison, but felt guilty when she immediately wished it had been Brian.

After a game in July, Izzy noticed Brian hadn't been talking to her like he used to. As he was about to pass by her on his way out, she stopped him and asked him if he was okay. He looked around the field, his eyes landed on

Jason, still in the dugout, and then he looked back at Izzy.

"You really like him?" Brian asked.

"I guess," she answered.

Brian nodded and looked down at the ground. Izzy knew something was bothering him and then wondered if it was the fact that she was spending time with Jason.

"Why?" she asked. "Are you jealous?"

Brian's head shot up and he snapped, "No!" Then he made a face and said, "I don't know."

Being too young and inexperienced in how to handle matters of the heart, Izzy had no idea what to do, so she did nothing. She stood there, her heart racing, waiting for Brian to say something else.

After a few seconds of silence, he said, "Whatever. It doesn't matter."

At that moment, Jason came rushing up behind her. "Hey, Izzy, I can't stay. Mom's picking me up. We gotta go to my aunt's. I'll see you later." He kissed her on the cheek and trotted toward the parking lot.

Izzy watched him go and then turned back to Brian. She still didn't know what she should be doing or saying. She walked to the bleachers and sat down. She started to play with the tiny silver ring on her pinky finger. She wasn't even sure what was happening. Out of the corner of her eye, she saw Brian walk over, hesitate and then sit down beside her. They sat in silence for a few minutes.

Izzy was the first to break it. "What doesn't matter?" she asked.

"What?"

"Before, you said it doesn't matter. What doesn't matter?"

Brian shifted positions and picked at the lace on his glove. "Nothing. You like Jason. Whatever. It's cool."

"Okay. Why do you seem mad?"

Shaking his head, he turned his body toward her and said in a rush, "Because I was going to ask you. I didn't know Jason liked you." Brian hesitated. "Or that you liked him." He shrugged.

"You were going to ask me what?"

"If you want to go out with me. But it doesn't matter now."

Izzy looked down and quietly said, "You should have asked." She looked back at Brian.

Brian stared at her for a few seconds and then said, "He got to you first."

At that moment, Izzy thought about breaking it off with Jason but she didn't want to hurt him, even if she did like Brian more.

"Yeah, I guess he did," she replied.

"Everything okay, here?" They looked up to see Brian's mom standing a few feet away.

Brian jumped up. "Yeah, I was just. . .uh. . .I was. . ."

"He was helping me figure out a problem," Izzy jumped in.

His mother smiled. In retrospect, it was the kind of smile that indicated she knew what was happening but wasn't going to embarrass her son.

Brian mother walked over, put a hand on Izzy's shoulder and said, "Well, I hope he was helpful and, whatever it is, I hope you go about it with kindness."

Izzy watched as Brian walked to their car with his mom. She didn't know what to make of what was just said. It wasn't until much later that she realized his mother knew Brian had a crush and was giving her some friendly advice.

Izzy continued to spend time with Jason, though often caught herself locking eyes with Brian after the games. She knew she had to do something. Claire helped her work up the courage to break it off. As it turned out, she didn't have to go through with it. The next day, Jason broke it off with her after announcing his family was moving and three weeks later, they were gone.

It didn't take long for Brian to ask her out after Jason ended it and the last weeks of that summer were spent at games, the arcade and Winding Lake.

"Your mom was so sweet," Claire's voice shook Izzy from her memories and she once again tried to focus on the present.

Brian noticed and nudged her, "Where'd you go off to?"

Izzy laughed, "Talking about your mother took me back to those summer baseball games when we were in middle school. She was your own personal cheer section. It was great."

"Yes, she was," Brian agreed.

"Izzy was a close second," Claire added.

Brian laughed, "Except for one summer, but only because he got to her first."

Izzy gasped. "That was the summer I was just thinking about." She saw Brian's eyebrows raise and then a sheepish smile cross his face.

"Who got to who?" Claire asked.

"Jason," Izzy replied.

"Oooh, yeah," Claire said. "I remember him. I remember sitting in your room planning out how you were going to break it off."

"Yeah, well, I didn't have to. They moved and the rest is history."

"Hmmm, I guess it is history," Brian said.

Their eyes met and Izzy tried to read what was in them when an uncomfortable thought crept into her brain. She glanced at her watch.

"Hey, it's getting late. Don't you have to check in with the missus?"

Brian cleared his throat and took a beat before answering. "No. I'm divorced."

TWO

"That boy has aged well," Claire said as she leaned on the counter, watching Izzy close out the register.

Izzy hadn't been able to think of anything else the entire day. The night before had been almost surreal to her. It still didn't seem real that Brian was back. After high school, he went to college in Ohio. She hadn't seen him since his college graduation party. They had ended things during his winter break sophomore year. Deciding that a long-distance relationship wasn't working, they'd gone their separate ways. They had kept in touch for a while, but then eventually she started seeing Ethan and Brian had found himself a girlfriend. The texts and emails stopped after that. The graduation party had been friendly, if not a bit awkward.

She had studied locally, and then had gone on to open the book store. Willow's End was a small community, so she'd heard through the grapevine how he'd found a job near Dayton and, eventually, had gotten married. He was a part of her life here, but a part that was packed away in boxes with the rest of her high school memories. She never thought she'd see him again, let alone that he'd come back to their little hometown.

"Yes, he has aged well," Izzy answered Claire. "Fifteen years ago he was a skinny kid who would skateboard everywhere and now . . ." She paused. "Well, now . . ."

"Now, he's filled out and has an ass that won't quit," Claire finished. When Izzy laughed and shook her head, Claire continued, "Come on! Don't tell me you didn't notice. I saw you checking him out."

"I'm not gonna argue," Izzy replied with a smile, "I checked him out. How could I not?" She closed the register drawer and zipped up the bank bag. "He's changed a lot. He's not the same, but yet, in some ways he is. He's still that same guy that used to make me laugh and I can still see the Brian I knew."

"I can't believe he's divorced. Who would let go of that?" Claire backed up from the counter. "Are you done here? Let's get a drink before I have to get home."

Izzy locked up the store and the two began walking down the street to Misty's Pub. "Isn't Greg going to wonder where you're at?" Izzy asked.

Claire shrugged. "If he's home. He's been working a lot of overtime lately. That highway project is behind schedule. They're hoping to start it next month but that's not likely. More like next year. Although, when it's done, it's going to bring some badly-needed business into this little berg."

"More business would be nice," Izzy replied, "but I don't want this town to become a tourist spot. It's fine just the way it is. The few people that come and stay at the inn are enough for me."

"Think bigger, my dear Izzy. We're a sleepy, quaint seaside town that some people like to visit. We've got one hotel - I mean, we've got one inn - that's right along the ocean. It doesn't even get booked to capacity in the summer. That highway is going to make a difference. We're the kind of unspoiled town people love to come to. The more people that come, the more money this town makes. Don't you want that for your store?"

Izzy sighed, "Yes, of course, I do. I just don't want to see this town become too commercial, that's all."

Arriving at the pub, they made their way to a table and settled in. They filled the time with small talk about books and movies while they waited for Barb, the owner's wife who also served as waitress and bookkeeper.

"Hey girls," Barb greeted them as she came up to the table. "The usual? Two Long Island Iced Teas?"

"That'll do it," Claire answered. "Thanks, Barb."

"So," Izzy started after a brief silence, "do you think Brian's going to stay?" She saw the sly smile creep across Claire's face. "Don't start. I'm just curious."

"I don't know. He did say he works remotely, so it's possible he could stay. You know," Claire smiled again, "I remember after his graduation party - after you had started dating Ethan - I remember asking you what you would do."

"I remember," Izzy replied. "You asked me what I would do if he comes back."

"I didn't think it would take this long, but here he is. He's back."

"For now, anyway."

"Maybe for good."

Barb interrupted to deliver their drinks and add to the conversation she'd obviously been eavesdropping on. "Look, Izzy, I heard he's gonna buy his parents house. Marty said Brian got in touch with him and he's meeting him on Friday to go over details. I think his Dad was just gonna let him live there but, I don't know, maybe the brother wants money from it? Who knows."

"Well, if Brian does buy it, that should give Marty a good commission given what the housing market is like lately," Claire added. "That's prime real estate being only a block from the beach."

"Looks like he's back permanently, Izzy," Barb said. "And single." Barb raised her eyebrows and walked away from the table.

"Well, there's your answer," Claire said.

Izzy took a long sip of her drink and set the glass back on the table. The idea of Brian being permanently back in Willow's End made her happy, but it also filled her with apprehension. They were much different people than they were ten years ago. Claire had put the idea in her head of something happening between them and she did wonder if there was still a connection, but those thoughts were both premature and a little disconcerting.

As if Claire had been reading her mind, she sighed heavily and put both her hands on the table, forcing Izzy to look up at her. "So what if

27

he's divorced. You don't know the details. We've had this conversation a million times."

Izzy was unsure of what to say. If it wasn't Brian she would have told Claire that between him leaving Willow's End after college, and also getting a divorce, she wouldn't trust him to stay. But it *was* Brian and she couldn't say she didn't trust him. She wasn't even sure if she believed it, or if she used divorce as a reason to not take some of the dates seriously over the years.

She knew that with Brian what they had back then was young love, first love. It was fun and new. They had discovered and learned things together. He had been her first lover, and even though they had both been so young she remembered that first night so clearly. It was true when they said you never forget your first love. Izzy had always kept Brian in a special place in her heart. She'd never hold a divorce against him.

"Izzy, the majority of marriages end in divorce these days. Would you rather have people stay in an unhappy marriage? Life is too short to be miserable. Not all divorces are men leaving their wives high and dry."

"I know," Izzy sighed. "I think I was using that as an excuse to eliminate some of the men I ended up going out with. I don't know."

Claire didn't respond at first. She regarded Izzy for a few moments and then said, "Look, I know it was hard on you when Ethan left. I knew it took a while, and maybe you're still not completely over him. But the truth is you used a lot of excuses to get out of those dates. Granted," she paused and chuckled a little, "some of them were definitely worth getting out of."

"Oh, my God," Izzy laughed. "Remember the guy who took his iguana everywhere?"

"There were definitely some winners, gotta say." Claire shook her head and then grew quiet before she continued. "Seriously, though, I've often wondered if you were just comparing them all to Ethan or if there was something deeper happening?"

"Deeper?" Izzy gave her friend a confused look. "Deeper how? I thought I was going to end up marrying Ethan. I really thought that's where it was headed. I think . . . I don't know . . . maybe I was comparing. Ethan's smart and funny and . . ."

"And he's been gone for three years. Have you heard from him lately?"

The truth was Izzy hadn't heard from Ethan in a couple months. They had talked or texted almost every day in the first year after he left. It eventually dwindled over time until it was a call or a text every couple weeks. This past year, however, the texts had been fewer and farther between.

"Not since July, I think," she replied.

"You're not holding on to hope, are you? I mean he hasn't given you any hint that he will but what would you really do if he comes back? Do you think you could just pick up where you left off? Knowing he doesn't like it here?"

Izzy eyed her friend. She wasn't sure if she was holding onto hope or not. All she really knew is that she hadn't been interested in any of the men she had gone out with the past couple years, even the ones that had their lives together and didn't carry reptiles around. In response to Claire's question, she simply shrugged.

"Ethan's never given you any indication that he'll come back, Izzy. You barely hear from him anymore. That should tell you what you need to know. I've said this before - if he still wanted you in his life he would have come back for you by now. We've had this conversation so many times."

Picking up her drink, Izzy took another sip, then drained the glass and signaled to Barb for another one. "I know you're right," she said.

"I'm sorry," Claire replied, "Maybe that was harsh, but it's still true."

"It's fine, Claire. I came to that conclusion a long time ago. It's not wrong to still have feelings for him, though. I know I should have moved on. I just didn't feel it with any of those guys."

"That's fair," Claire replied. "Maybe Brian can help you feel it."

Izzy shook her head. "I'm not going to use Brian to get over Ethan. That's just wrong on so many levels." She straightened herself up and sighed. "Besides, we're both different people now. It was high school, for God's sake. I don't even know the person he is now."

"Then get to know him," came Claire's answer.

Izzy eyed her friend for a moment and then gave a little laugh. "Claire, this is all extremely presumptuous on our part. For all we know, Brian could have taken one look at me last night and decided he dodged a bullet."

"Oh, please. I saw the way he looked at you."

Once again, Izzy shook her head. "If it was anything, it was only memories of the past and seeing each other again."

Barb set Izzy's drink down in front of her. "Here you go, dear." She turned to walk away, then stopped. "Izzy, I saw Brian yesterday. If you don't make a move on him, I will. He may be a bit on the young side for me, but who cares? He did an excellent job growing up. Mmmm mmm."

"Barb!" Izzy laughed, then pointed to the man behind the bar. "I think Charlie might have something to say about that!" Charlie was the owner of Misty's and Barb's husband.

"Hell," Barb replied, "he'd never even notice I was gone." With that, she walked away.

Izzy gave Claire an amused look and they both laughed for a moment. "You know, I don't think I would put it past her."

"Oh, I don't know. She complains about Charlie a lot, but she loves him," Claire replied. "She is on to something, though. I'm sure she isn't the only one around that knows he's single and saw how fine he is now." She raised an eyebrow at Izzy.

Izzy didn't have time to reply as they heard Charlie bellow from the bar, "Well, looky here! The prodigal son returns. It took you long enough to pay us a visit!"

The girls looked up to see Brian walk toward the bar and shake hands with Charlie. The two men engaged in conversation as Claire glanced over at Izzy. Izzy's eyes hadn't moved from Brian. Her heart skipped a beat and she felt the butterflies return to her stomach.

"Don't tell me you're not feeling *something*," Claire chided her friend. "It's written all over your face."

Izzy didn't reply. She couldn't deny it as she felt the heat rise in her cheeks. Glancing over at Claire she only shrugged. Looking back at the bar, she watched Brian and Charlie deep in conversation. She assumed they were catching up with each other. Seeing Brian again brought up all the memories and all the feelings she'd had all those years ago. He had been more than just her high school boyfriend, he had also been her best friend. She thought back on all their conversations, all the times they confided in each other about everything from their feelings to their dreams.

"Like I said," Izzy said, pulling her eyes away from Brian and back to Claire, "it's a little premature talking about this. Who knows what his divorce was like or what he's thinking. I think you're jumping the gun a little bit."

"I'm just telling you what I see," Claire took a sip of her drink and then, "Besides, it's not like he's a stranger or carries a pet lizard around–"

"Iguana."

"Whatever. You guys were great together."

"When we were kids. We're grown ups now."

"And like I said before; get to know who he is now. What's the harm in that? There isn't any."

Once again, Izzy didn't reply. Her gaze went back to the bar as her mind went back to a long ago day when they were out at Winding Lake. Brian was skipping rocks across the water and she was sitting on the edge of the path, watching him.

Out of nowhere, she asked him where she thought they would be five years after graduation. He hadn't hesitated. He said they'd be a year out of college, so by then they'd be planning their wedding and looking for a house. She was both stunned and thrilled by his response. He looked perplexed and told her he didn't know why she'd gotten so excited since she should know they'd be together forever.

Forever. He was the first one to promise her a forever. Ethan had been the second. Neither one had delivered on the promise. Of course, Brian was only a kid of 17 when he made that promise, she couldn't exactly hold it against him.

Izzy dropped her gaze to her glass and said, "I don't know, Claire. He's only been back a couple days. Time will tell if he really plans on staying. It might be useless to even think about anything."

Claire hesitated before answering. "Are you sure there's not something deeper going on, Izzy?"

Izzy's head snapped up. "That's the second time you said that within a few minutes. Like what?"

"Well," Claire leaned back. "maybe there is a reason you weren't interested in anyone since Ethan left and why you seem to be talking yourself out of re-acquainting yourself with Brian."

Rolling her eyes, Izzy picked up her glass, then set it down again. "How about none of the guys sparked my interest? Not hard to understand. How about Brian's only been back what? 48? 72 hours? What do you want me to do? Jump him as he leaves the bar?"

"I'm sure he wouldn't mind," Claire gave her a devilish smile.

Izzy's mouth dropped and then the irritation she was feeling evaporated and she began to laugh. "I couldn't even if I wanted to."

Claire was about to ask if she was thinking about it and then a thought hit her. "Wearing your old lady underwear, are you?"

Unable to answer, Izzy simply nodded and the two friends fell into more laughter.

"Can you imagine?" Izzy asked after a minute. "After ten years, he comes back to find out I'm old fashioned and wearing granny panties."

Claire waved a dismissive hand. "Honestly, I'm not sure he'd care. Although, you might find a gift box containing red lacy ones the next morning."

"With a little note."

"Dear Izzy, you're not one of the Golden Girls. Love, Brian."

They laughed again and when it subsided, Izzy looked across the table and shook her head. "Oh, Claire, seriously though."

"Yeah, yeah," Claire ran a finger under her eye and continued, "you might be right that it's a little premature, but if he sticks around, you better jump on him. Oh!," Claire laughed again. "I meant . . . well, you know what I meant!"

Izzy dropped her head in her hands and chuckled again. When she looked up, she took a deep breath and said, "*If* he sticks around."

"Oh, girl," Claire replied, "there's only one way to find out if he is . . . spend time with him."

Izzy was about to reply when she noticed Brian's conversation with Charlie had ended and he was headed their way. Her heart began to beat faster and she realized she was a little nervous.

If He Comes Back

THREE

"That's the beauty of starting your own business and being an IT consultant," Brian was explaining to Claire. "I can pretty much work from anywhere. Sometimes I have to go on-site but not every often."

Brian had heard their laughter and found a polite way to end his conversation with Charlie. He took his drink and asked the girls if he could join them. The conversation had started out light-hearted about random subjects until Claire decided to fish around and find out if Brian planned to stay in Willow's End.

"Okay, that's cool," Claire replied, "so do you plan on working from here permanently, then?"

Izzy noticed Brian shift in his chair and picked up what she thought might be uneasiness. "Hey, did you hear about the highway?" She chimed in. "They're expanding 44 with an off ramp that will come pretty much next door to here. Claire thinks it will bring in more vacationers."

Brian looked over at Izzy with a small smile. "Yeah, I heard. That would be great for the businesses in town, including yours."

"It will be, except I'm worried about this place becoming too commercialized."

"Yes," Claire interjected, "she'd like to keep this town in a time capsule, apparently." Turning toward Izzy, she continued. "There's nothing wrong with expanding, Izzy. This place can use some new life."

"I understand what Izzy means," Brian replied. "The charm of this area is that it's authentic. The old buildings haven't been torn down to make room for modern, sterile, glass and steel garbage. It has that old, small-town feel where a person can breathe in open spaces instead of being inundated with neon lights and big stores."

"Exactly!" Izzy said.

"No one said the town itself had to change. I mean, we're not talking about putting a Walgreens on every corner. Maybe another hotel on the outside of town or convert the old shoe factory into a hotel." Claire argued.

"The shoe factory," Brian and Izzy said in unison and then looked at each other and smiled.

"Well, clearly, I'm missing something," Claire said and smiled. Looking at her watch, she continued. "Anyway, I gotta run. Greg's gotta be home by now, I'm sure. I'm actually surprised he hasn't called." She got up from her chair, pulled on her coat and gathered her things. "I'll call you later, Izzy," she said with a knowing smile as she left.

After watching Claire exit, Izzy turned to Brian. "You remembered."

"Our plan to bring culture to this town? Sure, I do," Brian replied. "I've actually thought about it on and off over the last couple years."

"You have?" Izzy was surprised.

Brian nodded. "If you think about it, it's still a good plan. The factory is in worse shape than it was when I left here, but it could still work. A restaurant on the bottom, art gallery on the second floor, apartments on the third floor so the rent from them would pay for the loan on the building. I'm surprised no one has done something like that already. You'd think Marty would be pushing to sell that building."

"I'm sure he's tried," Izzy replied. "We were what? Sixteen when we came up with that plan?" She shook her head and chuckled softly. "I remember the day we came up with it."

"Out by Winding Lake," Brian said, looking down into his drink. "You were going to find painters and photographers and fill the gallery with their work until you took art classes and painted your own to sell. I was going to learn how to cook French cuisine and be the master chef in the restaurant. We were going to make the entire fourth floor our own place so we could live and work in the same spot." He fell silent for a moment and then looked up at her. "The dreams of kids."

"It was a good dream," Izzy replied as she looked into Brian's eyes a moment longer than she should have. She felt her heart begin to race. She looked away, cleared her throat and began speaking again. "You're right, though. Someone else should have renovated that building years ago. I wonder why it never sold. It's a shame it's still vacant."

"Yes, it is," Brian answered. He hesitated a moment and then shifted positions, turning fully toward Izzy. "How have you been, Izzy? Don't give me the normal answers. I want to know. How have you really been?"

A little surprised by the question, Izzy took a moment to answer. "I'm okay, Brian. I mean, I'm sure you've heard Ethan left." She waved her hand around. "Small town and all that. But I'm okay. I've got my store, my dog and things that keep me busy."

"Do you miss him?"

"Yes," Izzy answered. For reasons that weren't clear to her, she began telling Brian her story. She told him everything, how her and Ethan had gotten together, how she felt about him, what their plans and dreams were, and ultimately, how he left. Without thinking about it, she even told him how she still thinks about him from time to time, how there were moments she wondered if she made the wrong decision by not going with him, and how there were days she had hoped he'd walk back into her store, but she knew that would never happen. She even recounted some of the dates she'd been on since.

After she was finished, Brian was quiet for a while. She wondered if she'd told him too much. "I'm sorry," she said quietly. "I guess that was more than you bargained for."

"No, it wasn't. It's what I asked. You were right, I did hear some things when I came back, but I wanted to hear how you were doing from you, not from others."

"And now you know," Izzy replied. "I'm fine. I just need to keep moving forward." Eager to move the conversation away from herself, she asked, "What about you? I told you my story, it's your turn to tell me yours."

Brian let out a short breath. "Not much to tell, really. Got my degree, got a good job, got married, got divorced, started my own business. That's it in a nutshell."

Izzy leaned in slightly and looked him in the eyes. She wanted to know the same thing he had wanted to know. "But how are you doing?"

He held her gaze for a few moments before responding. "It wasn't easy, Iz. I'll tell you that. I really did love her, or I thought I did, but I never should have married her. She gave me an ultimatum; I put a ring on her finger or we would break up. I didn't want to break up, so I put the ring on her finger."

Izzy's eyes were wide. "An ultimatum? Oh, red flag, Brian! Red flag."

"I know," Brian said. "My friends kept warning me. I didn't listen. They were right. Once she got me to the altar, she thought she could use that same tactic for everything else she wanted. There were always ultimatums; do this, do that, buy her this, buy her that or she was leaving. I took four years of it. Then one day she said she wanted to have a baby. The moment she said it was the moment it all became clear to me. She was not the person I wanted to have a child with. She was not the person I wanted to be tied to for the rest of my life. She said we either had a baby or she was leaving. I saved her the time and I left."

"I'm sorry, Brian," Izzy offered.

"Don't be," Brian answered. "It wasn't easy, but leaving was the best thing for me. It would have been worse if I had stayed. I saw in her only the things I wanted to see. I had blinders on for most of the marriage. When they came off, I saw how materialistic and superficial she was." He picked up his glass and tilted it toward her. "Always listen to your friends, Iz. They see things you're too blinded by love to see." He took a sip and set the glass down.

"So, the blinders came off, you made a decision that was best for you, but . . ." Izzy paused for a moment. "You're thinking about staying here now? In Willow's End?"

He made a motion toward the windows. "I lost myself out there. At college, in Dayton, in my marriage, I never really felt like myself. I never felt at home anywhere. It was a colleague of mine who told me to think of a place where I had once been happy and that's where I should go. So, here I am."

A warmth came over Izzy and she felt it in her cheeks. She knew she was a part of why he had been happy here. She hoped she wasn't noticeably blushing. She looked down at her

45

glass, unsure of how to respond in a mature way. After all, she reminded herself, there was more to his life here in Willow's End than just her. She had only been one part of it.

"Can I get you two anything else?" Barb had somehow materialized at their table.

Izzy checked her watch. "Oh, no. Nothing for me. I have to get home. I have to feed and let Jasper out. That poor boy is probably dancing around between having to pee and being hungry."

"Nothing for me, either. I should get going, too." Brian said as Barb gave them both a smile and went on to another table.

Getting up to get her coat on, Izzy paused and looked at Brian. "It was good to talk to you, Brian. I'm glad you came in here."

"We can still talk. Let me walk you home?" Brian ventured. Izzy nodded and gathered her purse.

After settling the tab, they walked out onto Main Street and headed in the direction of Izzy's house. The air was chilly and it was still damp from the afternoon showers they had, but Izzy barely felt it. She wasn't sure if it was the drinks or Brian or both, but she felt a warmth she hadn't felt in quite some time.

The conversation came easily as they talked about the town and their neighbors. Izzy caught him up on the latest news. They laughed as they reminisced about how some of the people in town had acted in high school, including the current chief of police, who had graduated a few years ahead of them. No one would have guessed that someone as rebellious as Tim Walker would end up being the person in charge of order in their little town.

"He is completely different now," Izzy said as they turned onto her street. "He's good at his job. It's amazing."

"That's because there's nothing that kids could think of to do that Tim hadn't either thought of or actually did himself. He knows what to look out for," Brian laughed.

"That's very true," Izzy replied.

As Izzy continued to interact with Brian, she found herself drawn to him in a way she hadn't experienced in years. His presence seemed to awaken something within her, igniting a sense of longing that she hadn't felt since Ethan left. The easy chemistry she and Brian had once shared resurfaced effortlessly.

Another memory came back to her. This one made her smile as she remembered the day she realized she could tell him anything and he

47

would listen. Not just listen, but also talk about whatever it was she needed to say.

It was a late spring evening, the air was unusually warm and they were in Brian's backyard drinking slurpees. The conversation started out about finals and which ones they were worried about. Eventually, Izzy grew quiet.

After Brian prodded her, she confessed she didn't feel she was as smart as he was. Looking up at the sky, beautiful in that moment between dusk and darkness, she took a deep breath and told him that she sometimes thought his parents didn't think she was good enough, smart enough for him.

Closing her eyes, she waited for a response. She thought he'd tell her that his parents were old-fashioned and it didn't matter what they thought, or, as she was hoping, he would tell her she was wrong and that they loved her. Instead, there was silence.

She opened her eyes and looked over at him. Brian was simply looking at her. He tilted his head, furrowed his eyebrows and shook his head, but still said nothing. Her eyes began to water and she thought it meant what she said was true.

Before the tears could fill her eyes, he quietly asked her if she thought *he* was good enough for *her*. Astounded, she told him he was and should never think he wasn't. Then she asked him how he could even ask that.

He replied by asking her how she could think she wasn't smart enough or that anyone would ever think she wasn't good enough for *anyone*. He went into detail of all the things he thought she excelled at. When he was finished, he looked her in the eye and asked her what she thought of herself. Did *she* think she was good enough?

It took her a moment before she could respond. What she assumed would be a simple statement and response had turned into something deeper. It caught her off-guard, but she told him she thought she was. He told her that wasn't good enough. He wanted to know what she believed.

When she hesitated, Brian asked, "I want you to tell me the truth, Iz. What do you really believe about us?"

Izzy paused for a moment and then said, "I believe we're good together. I believe we're good for each other. We believe in each other."

"And we believe in us," Brian smiled back at her.

That evening was so long ago but the memory was crystal clear. It became a core memory because of the way he had handled her obvious teenage insecurity. She discovered she could trust him with her thoughts and insecurities. Even as a teenager she knew how important that was.

As she looked at Brian now, talking easily about the town and their mutual friends, she wondered if there was a possibility that they could reconnect in that way again. Would she be able to trust him in that way again?

As they rounded the corner onto her street, Ethan crept into Izzy's mind. She began to wonder if he, too, would someday consider coming back to Willow's End. Then she wondered why Ethan was invading her thoughts at that moment, when she was enjoying her time with Brian. She pushed it away and refocused on Brian.

Izzy had to admit the years he had been away had been good to Brian. His eyes still had that sparkle that hinted at mischief, his laugh was still infectious. His muscles were more defined; it was clear he was working out, but he wasn't hard. She wondered if his hugs would feel the same. She imagined the feeling of being wrapped in a favorite, familiar blanket and feeling safe and protected at the same time.

They stopped in front of her house. Izzy fished through her purse for her keys, debating on whether or not she should ask Brian to come in. As she found them at the bottom of her bag, she decided it was too soon.

"Did you change your number?" She heard Brian ask.

"No," she smiled. "It's still the same."

"I'd like to see you again, Izzy, maybe get to know more about the last decade of your life."

"I'd like that, too," she replied.

Brian looked around. "I have to say, it feels kind of good being back here."

"Kind of?"

Tilting his head and raising his shoulders just a bit, Brian replied, "Well, it's a little strange, too. I've walked these streets a thousand times. I know every inch of this town." He paused for just a beat. "I'm not gonna lie. There was a time, in college and a little after, that I didn't want to come back here. Funny how things change. Funny how time . . . and life . . . give you a little perspective. It feels good to be back, but . . ." He trailed off.

"But?" Izzy prompted.

Brian shook his head. "Nothing," he replied. "I guess it'll just take a little time to adjust to being back, that's all."

"That's if you stay," Izzy said.

Brian narrowed his eyes and considered Izzy for a second. "There's a lot up in the air right now. There's a lot of things I'm considering."

Izzy nodded. Unsure of how to reply to that, she pointed to her house, "I have to get inside. Jasper's waiting."

They said their goodbyes and Izzy let herself into her house. She peeked through the curtain on her door and watched him as he walked back down the street. Jasper wouldn't let her linger, though, as he jumped on her and ran to the back door. She followed him, let him into the back yard and got his dinner ready for him.

When he came back in and was eating, Izzy began petting him. "What do you think, buddy?" As if he understood what she was saying, Jasper looked up and snorted at her. "I don't know what that means, my boy. All I know is that it was good being with Brian tonight." She sat down next to him as he continued his dinner.

Tonight did feel good, she thought. Time seemed to have slipped away. She felt comfortable with Brian, back in the same kind of groove. Yet, it troubled her that he hadn't mentioned he was thinking about buying his father's house. She took that to mean he was unsure if he was staying in Willow's End, that there was a very real possibility this was just a visit.

Claire had given her the idea that maybe something could happen between them again. She had to admit it made her happy thinking about it. But now she wasn't sure if that was a possibility. Maybe he was just looking for a friend, an old friend he could confide in while he was here. If that was the case, she could be that friend, she thought. She would always be there for Brian, even if it was just to listen.

Her phone dinged and she retrieved it from her back pocket. She leaned against the wall and smiled as she read the text.

I'm glad you didn't leave Willow's End.

Smiling, she typed in her reply.

And I'm glad you came back.

If He Comes Back

FOUR

It had been a busy day in the book store. It usually did pick up in late October as more people came in looking for ghost stories, books on the paranormal or books about practicing witchcraft. Everyone seemed to become a novice witch around Halloween. It always amused Izzy.

Her cashier, Liza, was checking someone out as Izzy carried another carton to the counter. She tore the tape off and was emptying the new books onto the counter when she heard the jingle of the front door. She looked up to see Carol Bowen walk in. Carol and her husband, Frank, owned the Willow Inn, the only hotel in town.

"Hi, Carol," Izzy called to her. "Anything I can find for you today?"

Carol spotted Izzy and walked over to the counter. "I hope so, Izzy. I'm looking for the latest Stephen King. Do you have it?"

"If you're talking about *You Like It Darker*, no. We sold out. He sells fast this time of year. I do have a few *Holly* left and I think one *Fairytale*."

"Oh, I'll take *Fairytale*. I haven't read that one yet. Will you get more of the new one in?"

Izzy walked from behind the counter and over to the horror section of the store. "Yes, we'll get more in. It may not be until next month for the new one, though." She found the book and returned to the counter. "I can call you when it arrives."

"That would be wonderful, thank you," Carol replied. "I shouldn't read these books during the off-season. The inn makes all kinds of noises when it's empty."

Sliding the book over to Liza to check out, Izzy said, "It won't stay empty for long. You'll get the usual Thanksgiving and Christmas people coming. And you always do such a wonderful job with the annual Christmas gathering. It'll be a warm and cozy place again before you know it."

"Oh, I know. Besides, it's not *completely* empty right now. You know we have Brian staying with us. Though I'm not sure why he isn't staying with his father. He said something about cleaning it all out. He's such a good man." Carol almost whispered the last sentence.

Izzy already knew where Brian was staying. Everyone did. That was definitely one of the downfalls of living in a town this size. Everyone knew everything as soon as it happened.

She also knew that several people they had gone to school with had been there to see him since she'd seen him only a few days ago. Several of the guys he hung out with in high school had gotten him out for a night of pool and beer. She also knew Brooke had been there.

Brooke Mason – beautiful, high school valedictorian and a widow. Brooke's husband had been killed in a car accident on I-95 involving a tractor-trailer. Izzy had always liked Brooke and had been there for her after the accident, as most of the town had been. She couldn't help herself, though. A twinge of jealousy about the visit resided in her and she knew she had no right to feel that way. She kept trying to push it aside since she'd found out about it.

"I know he's staying with you," Izzy answered Carol. "He's in IT. He might be able to help you and Frank with your Wi-Fi while he's there. You might end up with more guests jamming it soon."

Carol rolled her eyes. "I know, the highway, blah, blah. We'll see. It would be great for business but I have to say, I'm not looking forward to more city people coming in. They're so rude these days. It's as if everyone forgot their manners." She reached out and took Izzy's hand. "But, honey, you better snatch that one up again. I'm telling you, he's not going to stay single for long. In fact, he makes me wish I was 30 years younger." She giggled at herself and let go of Izzy's hand.

Liza, who was ringing up the sale, snorted at Carol's comment and then looked at Izzy. "Sorry, but that was funny. He makes her wish she was 30 years younger and he makes me wish I was older. He's hot, Izzy, in case you didn't notice."

"Apparently, everyone has noticed," Izzy answered, thinking of Brooke. Turning her attention back to Carol, she said, "Ask him about the Wi-Fi. I'm sure he'll help you."

"I will," Carol said as she took her bag. "Don't forget to call me when the new book comes in."

Izzy was about to reassure her when the familiar jingle interrupted them. All three looked over as Brian made his way into the store. He looked over, saw the three of them staring at him as if they'd just been caught committing a crime, nodded his head and walked toward the self-help section.

"Well, that wasn't too obvious," Liza said as Izzy leaned on the counter and put her head in her hands.

Carol patted the top of Izzy's head and said, "Think about what I said, Izzy. I won't ask him about the internet right now. I'm sure he came here with other things on his mind." She poked Izzy's shoulder for effect. "Gotta run. Frank's going to want his dinner soon."

"Bye, Carol," Izzy muttered to the woman's retreating back. Sighing, she straightened up and continued what she had started before Carol had walked in. She realized her hands were slightly shaking. When all the books were out, she broke down the box and took it into the back room. Taking a deep breath hoping to get rid of the butterflies that had once again inhabited her stomach, she turned to go back to the floor. She was almost back at the counter when she remembered she hadn't grabbed the sale stickers she had printed earlier that day. *This is ridiculous*, she thought to herself. *Pull yourself together. You're not in high school anymore.*

Back at the counter, she began placing the stickers on the books. She glanced up and scanned the room but didn't see Brian. Disappointment came over her as she thought he might have left when she had gone into the back.

She felt Liza nudge her and saw her lift her chin toward the gift area. Looking over, she saw Brian browsing the coffee mugs. Relief went through her. She heard Liza chuckle and Izzy elbowed her in the side. It only made Liza laugh louder.

"I need to use the restroom," Liza said as she quickly walked away from the counter.

"Good idea," Izzy answered.

Finishing the stickers, she stacked the books into two piles and was about to carry one of the stacks over to the table for new arrivals when she saw Brian looking at the paintings on the wall.

While she wasn't sure if any of her paintings were good, she had brought in a few and hung them up as decoration. Izzy noticed he had been studying the one of Winding Lake. Leaving the counter, she walked up behind him.

"Not the best representation," she said, "but at least people recognize it."

Without turning around Brian replied, "It's really good, actually. Is it for sale?"

"No," Izzy said a little too quickly, making Brian turn around with a quizzical look on his face. Izzy continued, calmly. "I mean it's there for decor purposes. None of the paintings are for sale, but if you want a picture of the lake there are some for sale over at Renner's. I think they even have them in poster size."

"I like this one," Brian answered. "I always preferred the lake over the beach and this seems to capture it exactly the way I remember it. Maybe I should talk to the artist. Who painted it?"

"She did." Liza called out. They hadn't noticed she had returned to the counter.

Izzy became slightly embarrassed and wasn't sure what to say, so she gave Brian a small shrug and smiled. Brian tilted his head. Izzy couldn't read the look on his face. Amazement? Pride? Surprise? She wasn't sure. He had known she was interested in painting, but she hadn't pursued it in high school. She only took the classes after Ethan had left. In the beginning, it was a way to fill the time, but now it was her way of opening up and being creative.

"You did it," Brian said with a big smile. "You said you wanted to learn. That's fantastic!" He turned back to the painting. "And this is excellent, Izzy. Seriously." Turning back to her, he asked, "You won't sell it?"

Izzy shook her head. "I don't sell my work. I do it for myself. I thought about it briefly, but they're like my kids in a way.

Besides, I really don't think they're good enough to sell."

"You're wrong," Brian replied, turning back to the painting. Almost too quiet to hear, he said, "There's something special about this one." He paused for a moment and then turned back to Izzy. "Are you sure you won't make an exception for this one? I'd really like to buy it."

Shaking her head, she replied, "Sorry."

"Okay," Brian answered. "Question - do you have time for a little walk?"

Izzy hesitated and then turned to Liza, "Can you-"

Liza cut her off, "Go. I got this covered."

Once outside, Izzy followed Brian's lead down Main Street and toward the edge of town. Just like before, the conversation came easily. She didn't pay attention to the turns they were taking as she was caught up in how comfortable she felt with Brian.

After nearly fifteen minutes she asked, "So, are we just walking and talking or is there a purpose for this walk?"

Brian smiled at her but did not answer her question, instead he asked her about her paintings. Izzy was more than happy to talk about the classes she took, how she wasn't sure she was good at it but she enjoyed doing it. She admitted the times she spent outside with her easel and Jasper were some of her most calming and happiest moments.

It wasn't until they were at the entrance to Winding Lake that she realized there was, indeed, a purpose for the walk.

"Why'd you bring me here?" She asked.

"I want to show you something," Brian answered.

Izzy followed as he started down the path to the lake. She couldn't imagine what he could possibly show her. She knew the lake backwards and forwards. This was the place she frequently came to, not only to paint, but often just to think or relax. There wasn't a part of this area that her and Jasper didn't know.

Brian stopped at the edge of the lake. He pointed to his left where a row of willow trees lined the lake. "Tell me what you see."

"I see the willows," Izzy said, confused.

"Okay, tell me what you *don't* see."

Izzy looked at the willows and the surrounding area. She wasn't sure what he meant but she didn't see anything out of the ordinary. "I don't know. Other people?" She shrugged her shoulders.

"Iz, I came out here the day after I got back. I noticed right away that two of the willows had been cut down." He pointed to the tree stumps. "I asked Marty. He said lightning got them about four years ago. You know what one of them was."

She knew, and realized she should have known what he meant when he asked what she didn't see. They had been feeling particularly silly one afternoon and decided to act like a couple from a rom-com movie. They skipped along the lake, spun around in the sun and chased each other around the trees. They ended their play-acting by carving their initials in one of the trees.

Izzy remembered the day they cut the trees down after the storm. She took a picture of their tree before the crew got to it. Ethan had questioned why she was so sentimental about it. She remembered thinking that he ought to know. He had only been two years ahead of them in school.

Ethan knew that her and Brian had been a couple and had spent many days out here. It was why he made their place the part of the beach where the sand gave way to the rocks. There were many times during the summer they would walk out there in the early morning, sit on one of the large boulders and watch the sunrise. She

64

hadn't watched the sunrise from the rocks since Ethan left.

Izzy had been sad the day the trees came down. After Ethan had asked her why she was so sentimental, she tried to hide it, brush it off, so he wouldn't think she was pining away for an ex-boyfriend. In hindsight, she thought that was exactly what she was doing.

"Izzy?"

Brian's voice shook her from her thoughts. "Yes, I do. I know what one of them was." She turned to him. "But why'd you bring me here to show me the stump? I've seen it a million times since it was cut down."

"Because it was cut down four years ago. Your painting, though. I saw the date in the corner. You painted that last year."

Izzy nodded, not sure what Brian was getting at. "I'm well aware of when I painted it."

"You painted in our tree. It wasn't here when you painted it, but you put it in. You didn't put the other one that was cut down in it, just ours."

Izzy fell silent. Her thoughts went back to the day she painted it. She had intended to capture the lake and the willows as they were. It had been early summer, the sun was shining and the flowers were in bloom. She thought she'd done a fairly decent job until she got home and propped it on an easel to finish the details. That was when she noticed what she'd done. It had been subconscious. She remembered smiling and thinking she must have been reminiscing. Liking the piece, she finished it, hadn't given the addition another thought, and ended up displaying it in her store.

Brian turned toward her. She felt herself turning to face him. Her thoughts were jumbled. She had easily written off adding in that willow to being sentimental and reminiscing, but maybe it was more than that. Maybe there was a part of her that never let go of him. She had been so wrapped up in missing Ethan, yet she had subconsciously painted in their tree. Was it possible Ethan wasn't the one she'd been missing?

"You see, Iz," Brian said quietly, "that tells me that I was still there, in your mind somewhere."

"Of course, you were," Izzy answered. "Like I could ever forget you."

Brian fell silent for a moment and then turned back toward the lake. "Do you still think about back then?"

Izzy laughed, "It's hard not to when this town is filled with a million reminders."

She watched as Brian shook his head and inhaled deeply. There was something he wanted to say, she was sure of it. She thought she knew what it might be, but she didn't want to be wrong. She felt like that middle school girl, back on the baseball field, not knowing what to say or do. This time, though, she was going to say something.

"Brian? What's on your mind?"

"I don't know, Iz," he turned toward her again. "You never really left my mind. Even after I got married. There were times that memories would come back to me and I would wonder . . ."

Izzy was fairly sure she knew what the end of that sentence would be but she didn't finish it for him. She let him gather his thoughts, as she gently laid a hand on his arm.

Brian gave let out a half-laugh. "I wondered a lot of things, to be honest." He glanced at the willow trees and then looked back at Izzy. "Seeing your painting, though, well, it showed me that I crossed your mind, too. At least a few times."

"More than a few," Izzy smiled.

Izzy saw him leaning in and hesitating. She gave a small smile to let him know it was okay. He bent his head and kissed her. She brought her arms up and put them around his neck. His arms encircled her waist. His kiss was as warm and electric as she had remembered.

FIVE

A week after the kiss by Winding Lake, Izzy and Brian found themselves once again walking toward it, only this time they had Jasper in tow. Admitting there was still a connection between them, they had agreed to take things slow. They decided they needed to get to know each other again - as the people they had evolved into over the years. Another thing they were in agreement on was they still had some healing to do from the way their prior relationships had ended.

Even given what they had agreed upon, they found themselves together every day over the last week. Their conversations alternated between telling each other things they had done while they were apart and reminiscing about the time they had spent together in their younger years.

As they reminisced about their shared memories and the adventures they had embarked on together, Izzy felt a sense of warmth and familiarity wash over her. She couldn't help but smile as she recalled the laughter they had shared, the secrets they had confided, and the dreams they had once dared to dream together.

In addition to their plan for the factory, they had also dreamed of the places they would travel to, the things they would see together and how they would grow old together.

But alongside the joy of reconnecting with her first love, Izzy had developed a sense of uncertainty. Over the previous days, she found herself thinking more and more about Ethan. Ethan never entered her mind when she was with Brian, but late at night, alone in her room with Jasper, Ethan would creep into her thoughts. If things with Brian were to progress, she needed to get Ethan out of her system.

She was beginning to feel torn between thoughts of Ethan, the loving and comfortable relationship they once had and the intoxicating pull she felt towards Brian, the man who had once held her heart so completely. The past and the present collided in a whirlwind of emotions, leaving Izzy confused. Logically, she knew the chances of Ethan coming back to Willow's End were slim to none. Especially since she hadn't heard from him for a while. Emotionally, though, that was a different story.

Even though thoughts of Ethan would fade away when Brian walked through the door, they would return again at night. Izzy was hoping the late-night thoughts would eventually fade away as well. She was beginning to think it was part of the healing process, but she had to admit that completely letting go of Ethan was going to be difficult. She had wanted to marry Ethan. The night before, she had admitted to Jasper that holding on to the hope of Ethan returning was what she had done for the last three years. She already knew he was a part of the reason she didn't take any of those dates seriously. Or that's what she was telling herself, at least. Some of the men were nice enough, and there were moments she questioned why she couldn't seem to connect with any of them.

On this evening, though, and at this moment, Ethan was not on Izzy's mind. She was feeling happy and relaxed as she and Brian took the familiar path to the lake and let Jasper off his leash to run. They settled on a bench and snuggled close as the setting sun brought a deeper chill to the air.

"He really likes coming here," Brian remarked as they watched Jasper run, then hop and circle along the bank of the lake.

"We both do," Izzy replied. "I like to paint here, as you already know. Sometimes I bring him out here just to relax and clear my mind."

"I like that you still came here over the years. I always thought of this as our place. It's funny," Brian let out a little chuckle, "this was the first place I came to when I got back."

Izzy turned her head and looked up at him. "I know you said you came here but I didn't know it was the first place you went. Why's that?"

Brian looked down toward the gravel in front of the bench. "Well, like I told you, I've thought about you a lot over the years, Iz. There were quite a few times I almost called you, but I didn't want to interrupt your life or make you uncomfortable in any way. So, I didn't. When I was on my way back, all these memories of you were going through my mind. I came here first because I wanted to see our tree. I wanted to see if you could still see the initials. I didn't know it had been cut down. I was sad to see that. I thought maybe that was some kind of omen that the past is the past and maybe should be left there." Turning to face Izzy, he said, "But here we are."

"Here we are," Izzy echoed. "Some things should stay in the past, that's true, but not everything." She smiled and gave him a kiss.

"Glad you feel that way," Brian hesitated as if there was something he wanted to say but then stopped.

"Is there more?" Izzy asked.

"No, I was just thinking, that's all."

"About?"

Brian smiled. "We were young, but you know what? Our dreams weren't as far-fetched as you'd think. I mean, we didn't dream about conquering the world or curing diseases or climbing Mount Everest. Our dreams were actually practical, when you think about it."

Izzy tilted her head and thought about it for a moment. "You're right," she said. "The traveling, the places we'd see, that's not outlandish at all." She shifted in her seat and snuggled closer.

"The factory," Brian added.

Izzy laughed. "Yes, the factory. You were right when you said it was still a good idea."

Jasper interrupted Brian. He was about to speak when the dog excitedly approached them, leaping up and placing his front paws on Izzy. Izzy lovingly embraced her fur baby and praised him for being a good boy.

The dog jumped off and ran out on the grass. He began leaping and circling in the air, as if showing off to his human. Izzy and Brian laughed at the dog hamming it up. It wasn't long before Jasper was distracted and found a stick.

Walking excitedly back to the bench, Jasper wagged his tail in anticipation, looking back and forth between Izzy and Brian.

"I got this," Brian chuckled as he grabbed the stick from Jasper's mouth and walked onto the grass, Jasper jumping and barking at his heels.

Izzy watched Brian playing with Jasper. A feeling of peace and contentment came over her. As she observed him, her heart swelled with warmth, banishing the autumn chill. A smile spread across her face, her cheeks flushing with delight. Although she thought Brian had gotten more handsome over time, she could still see the boyishness in his face. It had a charm that was enchanting to her. She could simultaneously see the man he had become and the young boy he'd once been. She had loved that boy, and now she realized her feelings for the man were growing stronger.

The realization struck a different chord in her. It felt like momentary panic and she took a quick intake of breath. Her hand came up to her throat as she exhaled slowly. The feeling scared her. She didn't understand where it had come from. It began to subside, though, as she saw Brian walking toward her with his easy, relaxed gait and the smile that lit up his eyes.

Exhausted from chasing Jasper, Brian resumed his seat next to Izzy and wrapped his arm around her. "I swear nothing wears that dog out," he chuckled.

Not knowing exactly why, Izzy turned to him and asked, "Do you like being back here?"

Brian titled his head in confusion. "Of course, I do. I thought I made it clear that night at Misty's. This is my home."

"Yes, but you also said things were up in the air."

"Not anymore."

Izzy nodded, and then another thought that seemed to come out of nowhere came out. "I heard Brooke went to see you at the inn when you came back."

"Yeah, quite a few people did," he paused and laughed. "I forgot how fast word spreads around this town. It was great to see everyone again, though. I'm glad they came when they heard. It saved me from looking them all up again."

"I'm sure Marty and Tim and a few of the other guys wanted to catch up. You and Marty were pretty close back in the day. I'm sure he's glad you're back. I was just curious what Brooke wanted."

Brian looked at Izzy out of the corner of his eye, his eyebrows furrowed. "Why?" he asked and then he laughed. "Are you jealous?"

Izzy gave a small shrug. "I was just curious, that's all."

Brian sighed. "I'll be honest, it was good to see her. She's a good person. It's upsetting what happened to Joe, though. You can tell it still affects her. If you want the whole truth, she did ask me to go out for dinner sometime, but I politely declined. Is that what you wanted to know?"

Shifting in her seat, Izzy took a moment before responding. "I guess so. I like Brooke, and yes, she's a good person. When I heard she went to see you, I just wondered about it." She paused, then decided she needed to be honest with Brian. "Okay, no, that's not entirely true. Yes, I felt a few jealous pangs."

Brian laughed again and Izzy gave him a slight slap on the shoulder. "I find it cute that you were jealous," he said, "as long as, you know, it doesn't turn into that crazy kind of jealous where you carry a kitchen knife around with you and stalk any girl that looks at me. That would be a problem."

"Well," Izzy chuckled, "if that's a problem for you then don't look in my purse."

Brian laughed and hugged her tighter. "Oh, Iz, you haven't changed. You can still find a comeback to anything. I missed that. It's not the only thing I missed, but it does rank up there."

Izzy snuggled in tighter, she had also missed the back-and-forth banter. Ethan didn't always appreciate her comebacks. She felt better, but a little uneasy as she wasn't quite sure why she'd asked the last few questions. *What's wrong with me*, she thought. *This is good. Are you looking for a problem? Just stop it.*

Brian seemed to notice the slight change in her. "You okay?"

Izzy's mind went back and forth in a split second. She thought about being honest with Brian and telling him about the conflict that had arisen in her the last few days, but then realized it would probably upset him. She didn't want to ruin what was developing between them. Once again, she tried to chalk it up to the healing process.

"It's nothing," she answered.

"Did Brooke coming to see me really bother you that much?" Brian asked.

Relieved that Brian thought that was it, she shook her head. "No," she said, "I admit that it bothered me when I heard about it, but it's fine. She's a friend. We were all friends back then, so why wouldn't she want to see you? It was stupid of me to be bothered by it."

"Not stupid," Brian said, "just human. Besides, it makes me feel good that it bothered you."

Izzy let out a chuckle, sat up and looked at him. "Don't go getting a big head about it."

"I'm not," Brian answered, "but now you know how I felt when I heard you started dating Ethan."

The smile faded from Izzy's face. "What?"

Brian shrugged. "I know we were broken up and I was at school but, yeah. I guess I thought that we'd get back together by the time I graduated, even though you told me . . ." He stopped.

Izzy stared at him for a few moments. "I didn't know that."

Laughing, Brian said, "Of course, you didn't. It's not like I was going to call you and say 'Hey, I don't like you seeing Ethan'. I don't think it would have made a difference at that point anyway, even if I had called you."

Instead of replying, Izzy snuggled closer, put her head on his shoulder and hugged him tighter. "What's past is past," she said after a few moments.

Brian kissed the top of her head and said, "The present is much better, anyway."

Back at Izzy's house, after dinner had been cleaned up, Jasper fed and Izzy had changed into cozy sweatpants and a sweatshirt, they snuggled on the sofa, surfing for something to watch on TV.

"Feel like a movie?" Brian asked, remote in hand.

"I don't know if I can stay awake for it, to be honest," Izzy replied.

With a short nod, Brian flipped to HBO Max and brought up an episode of *Friends*. "Then we'll watch your favorite show. I'm assuming you still watch it and can probably recite all the dialogue now."

Izzy turned to him, surprised. "Yes, I can," she said with a laugh. "I can't believe you remembered this, too."

"Are you kidding? All you talked about through the last season was Ross and Rachel getting back together. It drove me insane." Brian said with a laugh.

"Well, the writers were lucky they wrote her getting off the plane because I would have stormed their offices if they hadn't. Seriously. Well, me and a few million other people."

"Yes, I know. I remember it well. You were always a sucker for those big romantic gesture scenes. Even in movies. I also remember handing you tissues when they aired the finale."

"You never really liked this show, as I recall." Izzy said.

"Not when it was on TV, no. But it's grown on me over the years." He gave her a kiss. "Maybe because it reminds me of you."

Izzy gave him another kiss and blushed, before Brian said, "Or maybe it's because I realized how funny Chandler actually is and that sarcasm of his is golden."

Before Izzy could reply, the show's theme started playing and, in unison, they did the four claps that come after the first line of the song. Laughing, they hugged tighter and settled in to watch an episode, which turned into watching four of them.

As Brian was getting ready to leave for the night, coat in hand, standing at the door, he gave Izzy a kiss and asked, "So, are we Ross and Rachel or are we Monica and Chandler?"

"Oh, we're definitely not Ross and Rachel," Izzy laughed. "You're not that neurotic."

"Then could I *be* any more like Chandler?"

"Oh, my God," Izzy laughed. "I think you may have actually sounded like him. Now, get out of here, you big goof! And P.S., I'm still a sucker for romantic gestures."

"Well, that's good information to have," Brian said before kissing her good night.

After he left, Izzy locked the door, turned and leaned against it. She couldn't remember when she'd felt this happy. Turning again, she peeked through the curtains and watched Brian walk to his car and get inside. Jasper came up beside her and gave a little whine.

"Don't worry, Jasp," Izzy said. "We'll see him again tomorrow."

Izzy hummed as she let Jasper out in the backyard and then straightened up the living room and kitchen, laughing at the thought that she was doing exactly what Monica in *Friends* would do. Taking Jasper upstairs, she got ready for bed.

The feeling of happiness she had felt seconds earlier faded. This was the part of the day she was beginning to dread. She hoped she would fall asleep quickly before any thoughts of Ethan could find their way in and keep her awake again.

SIX

"It's only been a month, Claire. Do you understand what 'taking it slow' means?" Izzy was up to her elbows in getting Thanksgiving dinner ready. Even though Claire was helping her, the barrage of questions was becoming a bit much.

"It's not like I'm expecting an engagement, for God's sake," Claire replied. "I only want to know how it's going. You've been unusually quiet about it, Izzy, that's all."

Izzy knew Claire was desperate for details. After all, she had been confiding in Claire since they were kids. There wasn't anything Claire didn't know about her. This was different, however. She knew Claire was expecting her to say Ethan was a distant memory and Brian is all she wants. But she couldn't say it. Things were going extremely well with Brian. Even though they had decided to take things slow, as both still had some healing to do, they'd been spending a lot of time together. So much so that Izzy had been neglecting her hobbies, including painting.

She loved every minute she spent with Brian, but she'd be lying to Claire if she said she hadn't thought about Ethan. Ethan had never been far from her thoughts since the day he left, and while Ethan never crossed her mind when she was with Brian, he was still entering her thoughts at night. Lately, she began to wonder what would have happened if Ethan had come back instead of Brian. Would they have picked up again the way she and Brian had?

Guilt was beginning to take over. She knew Ethan wasn't coming back and she knew she needed to get over whatever was making her think about him. However, she was beginning to wonder if what was happening with Brian was real, if the feelings she was developing were real or if she was doing what she had told Claire she did not want to do: use Brian to get over Ethan. That thought, in addition to the fact that she still thought about Ethan, were making her feel a sense of guilt. She tried to work it out in her head late at night, when the thoughts of Ethan would surface. She'd sit up in bed and talk to Jasper, but it was a conversation she wasn't ready to have with Claire.

"Jesus, Claire, give it a rest," Greg said from the living room. "I swear, Izzy, she's already planning your wedding, don't let her fool you. You take it as slow as you want to. She doesn't need to know everything all the time."

"Shush, Greg," Claire replied. "No one asked you." Scraping the mashed potatoes out of the pot and into a bowl, she turned back to Izzy. "I'm just asking if everything is okay."

"Everything is okay, Claire. I promise. It's going well. It's going exactly as he and I talked about - easy and slow." Izzy reassured her friend.

It was true. She wasn't lying about that. They were indeed taking it slow as far as the physical side of the relationship went. Though they spent almost every day together, they had not made it into the bedroom. Brian hadn't so much as hinted at it, and Izzy was relieved as she wasn't sure she was ready. There was a part of her that felt it wasn't right yet. Whether that had to do with Brian or Ethan, she wasn't sure.

Claire nodded and smiled. "Good. What time is he coming?"

As if on cue, Jasper's head popped up from his bed, ears alert. He got up and scrambled toward the door, barking and spinning. It was a few seconds before the doorbell rang and the door opened. Brian bent down and greeted the dog, rubbing his ears and talking to him.

"There's your answer," Izzy said.

Izzy popped her head out of the kitchen and watched as Brian played with Jasper and then greeted Greg. She smiled, thinking it looked so natural for Brian to be here. Brian looked up and returned Izzy's smile. Even after a month, his smile still made her heart leap. It always had, and she was pretty sure it always would, regardless of the chaos that went on inside her mind at night.

Seated at the table, everyone full from the meal, Izzy sat back and smiled. It was the first holiday she had not spent as the third wheel in three years. While she had been spending the holidays with Claire and Greg since they got married, she had felt out of place without Ethan. Today, she felt comfortable, relaxed and happy. The conversation was easy as Greg and Brian caught up with each other, and began making plans to go hunting. Claire and Izzy had groaned. Deer meat was still something neither one of them could get used to.

"Jerky," Claire said. "I'll allow it only if you make deer jerky. It's the only thing I like."

"Of course, dear," Greg answered and then lifted his glass. "Once again, an absolutely wonderful Thanksgiving dinner. To Izzy."

"Thank you, Greg," Izzy said as they all lifted their glass.

"I can definitely sense a touch of your mother in your cooking," Brian said. "I remember her big Sunday dinners. They were fantastic." He paused and then asked, "How are your parents liking it down there?"

"Arizona agrees with them," Izzy replied. "They never come back." She played with her glass for a moment then sighed. "Yup. They retired, they left me up here and they never come back here. If I want to see them, I have to fly there." She paused for a second. "It's good, though. I talk to them frequently and I try to make a trip down every February."

"Yup," Claire interjected. "Every year when the rest of us are tired of winter and still suffering from seasonal depression, Izzy takes off for the desert and the sun."

"Is that jealousy I detect, Claire?" Brian asked with a chuckle.

"Yes!" Claire replied. "She always comes back looking rested and tan. It's not fair. I keep telling her she needs to take the rest of us with her, but she never listens."

"Fine," Izzy said. "I'll take you on the one coming up. You have four months to pack, and knowing you, it's gonna take you that long."

Claire laughed and paused for a second. "Or," she dragged out the word. "You could take Brian."

Izzy glanced over at Brian and tilted her head. "Maybe that's not a bad idea."

Brian smiled. "Maybe," he said as he got up and began gathering the plates. Izzy took his lead and together they cleared the table as Claire and Greg went to the living room to watch the football game.

They filled the dishwasher and were washing the pans when Izzy once again realized how easy it was to be with Brian. It felt like they had been hosting holidays for years instead of him being a guest who was helping her with the dishes. She liked the feeling. She leaned into it and ribbed him about helping her make the dinner next time.

Brian laughed. "Not unless you want Coq au Vin for dinner and crepes for dessert."

Izzy gasped. "You cook French food! Why didn't you tell me sooner?" Brian turned and gave her a small smile. Her thoughts went back to their long ago plan. They both had done something tied to the idea they had come up with so many years ago. "That's great, Brian. You realize, of course, you're going to have to cook for me now."

"Of course," Brian leaned over and kissed her lightly, his hands still in the dishwater. Then he lifted his hand and tapped her nose, leaving soapy bubbles on the end of it.

Izzy responded by whipping the dish towel at him. He sprayed her with water. She tickled his side. He backed up from the sink to get away from her, hands dripping. Izzy almost doubled over laughing. She had almost forgotten how ticklish Brian was. Anytime she had wanted to get the better of him, all she had to do was tickle his side.

"Still haven't changed," Brian laughed as he grabbed the dishtowel out of her hands and dried his hands.

"I don't know what's going on in there, but you guys are missing a hell of a game," Claire said from the living room.

"Coming," Izzy said over her shoulder as she walked to sink to let the water drain out. Brian came up behind her, wrapped one arm around her and put the dish towel out in front of her. She wiped her hands and then turned into his arms, wrapping her arms around him. "I'm glad you're here."

"Here for Thanksgiving or here back in Willow's End and back in your life?" Brian raised an eyebrow.

"All of the above," Izzy replied before kissing him.

Walking into the living room, Brian took a look at the TV. "Lions are beating the Cowboys?"

"Sure are," Greg answered. "Shocking, I know." The two began discussing the game and the current football season as Izzy sat on the loveseat next to Claire.

She felt Claire pat her leg and smiled at her. Claire gave her a short nod and smile before turning her attention to the TV. Izzy looked over at the men. A feeling of warmth came over her, but more than that, it was also a feeling of completeness. It was a feeling she hadn't felt in so long. As she watched Brian's animated gestures, she began to think all the doubts she may have had the last few weeks were foolish.

Taking a sip of the wine she'd brought with her from the kitchen, she relaxed deeper into her seat. Her thoughts wandered back to the comment about taking Brian to Arizona with her in February. The idea began to excite her. Her parents had always liked Brian, it would be a nice surprise for them but then a feeling of trepidation crept over her.

For reasons she didn't know, she hadn't told her parents she was seeing Brian again. Izzy talked to them at least twice a week, and she had mentioned he was back in town, but she hadn't relayed that they were together again. She didn't know why. Her mother would be happy about it, but she hesitated each time, even though she was happier than she'd been the last few years.

Izzy found the last month with Brian's return to Willow's End to be a wonderful dance between past and present. Each conversation was a step towards understanding the separate journeys they had walked the last ten years. It was as if they were able to pick up right where they left off, and yet they were still learning a lot more about each other.

The vibration from her phone interrupted her thoughts. With her free hand, she pulled it out of her back pocket. The moment she looked at the text, time seemed to freeze. Her breath caught in her throat and her heart seemed to stop. Ethan.

Just checking in. I'm sorry I haven't called lately. Things got crazy but I've been thinking about you. You're prob with Claire and Greg. I won't interrupt. I really miss you.

Izzy sat motionless, staring at the screen; her mind unable to process the text. She glanced up at Brian, grateful he was wrapped up in the game and not looking her way. Claire, however, nudged her. She turned to see Claire giving her a questioning look. Instead of answering the look, she handed her phone to Claire.

She watched as Claire's eyes widened as she read the text and handed the phone back. Claire mouthed 'Are you going to answer that?' Izzy shrugged and mouthed 'I don't know'. Claire mouthed 'Don't' and tilted her head toward Brian.

Izzy leaned a bit closer and whispered, "We'll talk about this later. Not now."

Claire closed her eyes and shook her head. Then she looked back at Izzy and said in a normal voice, "Looks like we both need more wine." She grabbed Izzy's hand and took her into the kitchen.

"Don't answer that," Claire said when they were out of earshot.

"I'm shocked he sent it, Claire. I have no idea how to take it or what I'm going to do," Izzy replied.

"Jesus Christ, Izzy. I'm so tired of repeating myself with this. He's not coming back here. If he really missed you that much, why didn't he stay in touch? Why hasn't he come back to visit you? I said it many times before and I'll say it again - if he really wanted you he would have come back for you."

"Stop, Claire. I know."

"Do you? Because you have a good thing going with Brian. If you answer that text, you're asking for trouble."

Izzy eyed Claire for a moment. "Not necessarily."

"Yes, necessarily," Claire answered. Then she took a deep breath. "Izzy, just think long and hard about it. It might seem innocent to answer it but what good will it do?"

"I'm not going to answer him right now. Just let me process this. I *will* think about it. I'm not a child."

"I didn't say you were," Claire answered. "I just think you need to sort out your issue."

Izzy was taken aback for a moment. "Issue?"

"Brian is *here*, Izzy. He's making plans. He's going to buy his father's house."

"And?" Izzy wasn't sure what that had to do with her 'issue'.

Claire sighed. "Never mind. Just be careful and take time before you decide what to do about that text." With that, Claire took her wine and headed back to the living room.

Izzy hesitated a moment before following Claire back to the sofa. She was a bit irritated, not knowing exactly what issue Claire thought she needed to sort out. She was well aware Ethan had given no hint of coming back to Willow's End. Part of the reason she was taking it slow with Brian was because she needed to resolve Ethan leaving. She was doing that, she thought. What other issue was there?

Though she had to admit, the text didn't do much in the way of helping her resolve things. Maybe that's what Claire meant. It did come out of nowhere and whether she wanted to be honest with herself or not, the last sentence did give her a jolt and not in a bad way.

But why now, she thought to herself. It had been months since she'd heard from him. Why now, when, as Claire said, things were going really well with Brian. She felt as if her late-night thoughts had conjured the text in some way. Then a thought struck her - was this the universe's way of telling her something?

Her mind began to wander. She wondered where Ethan was spending Thanksgiving and who he was with. She pictured him at a table with people she didn't know, wondering what it was that prompted his text, what it was about this day that made him realize he missed her.

For the first time, the conflicting emotions she felt were happening while Brian was here with her. She cast her eyes down and tried to will all thoughts of Ethan away, but they wouldn't go easily. Her mind kept returning to the fact that wherever Ethan was and whatever he was doing, he was thinking about her.

Glancing at Brian, Izzy decided she wasn't going to respond to Ethan. It had been a good day. She thought maybe she'd respond tomorrow or maybe she'd listen to Claire and not respond at all. She decided to see what tomorrow brought. Then a thought crept into her head. She tried to will it away but it insisted on worming its way in. Ethan was missing her. If he was missing her, did that mean he still had feelings for her?

If He Comes Back

SEVEN

Balancing on the ladder, Izzy was trying to finish putting up the Christmas decorations in the store. She had finished the tree and placed it in the center of the store, now she was hanging snowflakes from the ceiling. It had been a couple of days since Ethan's text. Izzy had not responded to it yet and Ethan hadn't sent anything further.

She had finally confided in Claire about everything; her relationship with Brian, her late-night thoughts and the struggle she was having about whether or not to respond. Claire had been a supportive listener, empathized with her, but in the end she made a strong case for Brian, as Izzy had expected.

Izzy couldn't argue with anything Claire had said. Everything in her told her that Claire was right. Except her emotions. Izzy couldn't shut them off. Every time she thought about Ethan her mind went back to how they used to be, and she would be lying if she said she didn't feel something. When she was with Brian, she was happy and felt a peace she hadn't felt in years. The confusion was making her head spin. She was fairly certain she'd come to a conclusion about responding to the text, though she kept second guessing herself.

Hearing the jingle of the door, she glanced over to see Claire coming in. She waved and finished hanging the snowflake. Climbing down from the ladder, she moved it over a few feet and started back up, another snowflake in hand. Claire leaned against one of the bookcases and took off her gloves.

"How are you doing today?" Claire asked.

"I'm okay," Izzy answered. "Keeping busy, keeping my brain occupied."

"Are you hoping your subconscious works it out and you'll suddenly have an answer?"

Izzy looked down at Claire and snickered, "Something like that. It would be nice but it doesn't seem like my subconscious is cooperating." She hung the snowflake, climbed back down the ladder, took a seat on the bottom rung and stretched out her legs. "I gave it a lot of thought, Claire, and I think I'm going to respond to Ethan." She saw Claire open her mouth to speak, but held up a hand to stop her. "I think I need to talk to him. I need to know where his head is. It's been a while since he said he missed me. If he's saying it now, then maybe . . ." She trailed off.

Claire was silent as she walked over, got on the floor opposite Izzy and leaned against the wall. She played with her gloves for a few moments and then looked her friend in the eyes. "You're going to hurt Brian. I think you're scared and you're going to intentionally sabotage your relationship with him."

Izzy was surprised. She wasn't sure how to respond at first. Thinking Claire was going to be supportive of her decision, she wasn't expecting such a blunt answer. She took a long pause before answering. "Yes, I'm scared. I *am* scared I'm going to hurt Brian, but I'm also scared that if I don't get in touch with Ethan, I'll never know . . ." She fell silent.

"Know what?" Claire asked. "If there's still a chance? He doesn't want to live here, you don't want to move. Besides that . . ." Claire paused. "Never mind. Just that fact alone should be enough for you."

"Like I said, maybe I just need to know where his head is. Ethan and I had a good thing, too, Claire. Maybe the universe is trying to say something."

Sighing, Claire folded her arms across her chest. "Or maybe you're taking what it's saying the wrong way. Izzy, stop it. You're romanticizing your relationship with Ethan. You have barely heard from him over the last year. He sends you one sentence and you're holding on to it like it holds the key to your entire future. It's all based on the relationship you had with him years ago that you've built up in your mind as perfect. It wasn't. You'll get hit with reality *and* you'll lose Brian. Is that what you want?"

Stinging from Claire's words, Izzy's mouth had dropped open. When they had first discussed everything, Claire had been sympathetic. Even when she made her case for Brian, she had done it while still taking into consideration her feelings for Ethan. Today, it seemed Claire was bordering on belligerent and she didn't understand it.

"Is this your version of tough love?" she asked Claire.

"Someone has to do it," Claire replied. "I love you, Izzy, but you have to see what you're doing. I'm not going to say your relationship with Ethan wasn't," she paused for a moment as if looking for the correct word, "fine. For the most part, I guess it was okay. Then he chose not to stay and you chose not to go with him. He might not even be the same person anymore. Instead of moving forward, for three years you were stuck in the mud, spinning your wheels.

You didn't take any date you went on seriously and you kept your relationship with him alive - in your *mind*. Now you have something real, something tangible, something that is really good, and you're going to throw it away for what? Something you've built up in your mind that may not exist anymore? Someone who may never come back? What are you so afraid of?"

"First," Izzy started, "I'm not throwing anything away. I told you, I'm confused. I have an inner fight with myself every single night. I know how I feel when I'm with Brian. I can't even describe it. But then Ethan finds his way back into my mind. It's not something I can control, Claire. Second, I wanted to *marry* Ethan. That's not something you get over easily. And what did you mean our relationship was *fine for the most part*?"

"Like I said earlier, I think you romanticize it. I think you remember all of the good things, all the things that made you feel loved, and none of the things that you complained about. None of the things you were valid in complaining about."

"Every relationship has its ups and downs, you know that," Izzy replied. Claire did not answer, she only raised an eyebrow. Izzy sighed and did not continue. She began playing with the ring on her little finger, a habit she'd

101

had since childhood when she was feeling unsure of herself. After a few minutes of silence, she looked back at her friend. "I loved him, Claire."

"I know that you think you did," Claire answered softly.

"Why are you like this today? You know I did. You were there."

"Yes, I was," Claire answered. "I'm only trying to get you to really think back on things as they really were. Not just the good times."

Izzy put her head in her hands and thought about what Claire had said. Maybe she had been romanticizing the relationship. She hadn't considered that before now. It was true Ethan might be a completely different person now. It was also true she would have no way of knowing that since his communication had been very minimal. She should be angry at that, but Claire was right. Izzy was stuck on that one sentence in his last text.

Claire must have surmised what Izzy was thinking because the next thing she said hit Izzy hard. "If he really missed you, he would have called you instead of texting. If he really missed you, he would have said it long before now."

Lifting her head, Izzy felt her eyes water, though the tears did not fall. "You're right. I know you're right, and yet. . ." She took a breath. "Why can't I let it go?"

Claire closed her eyes and sighed. "Because you. . ." Claire stopped, shook her head and opened her eyes. "I can't give you the answer, Izzy. If I tell you what I'm thinking, you'll reject it. You have to figure it out for yourself, honey." Claire got up from the floor and pulled Izzy to her feet. "You're smart. The answer will come to you."

"Tell me what you're thinking, Claire. I need to know."

"If there's one thing I learned, it's that when it comes to matters of the heart, it doesn't matter what other people see or know. A person is going to do what they're going to do regardless of the red flags everyone else might see."

"What red flags? Tell me. I don't see anything to be concerned about with Brian."

"I don't see red flags with Brian, Izzy."

"How can you see red flags with Ethan? You haven't seen him for years."

"Because they're the same red flags that were always there. Like I said, you're a smart person. You'll figure this all out. I have to run, though. We'll talk tomorrow. Love you, girl."

Izzy gave her best friend a tight hug, thanked her for her honesty and then sent her on her way. She had to lock up the store and get home to Jasper. Brian wasn't coming over tonight. He had moved into his father's house, but there were still things that needed to be settled, although he'd been vague about what needed to get done.

In fact, Brian had been vague more than a few times lately. He'd be late getting to her house, or he'd back out of lunch. Each time he said it had something to do with moving into his father's house. She believed him, she just didn't understand why he became so vague when she would ask him what needed to be done. She said she could help him, but he'd decline her help, saying it was just easier to do it all himself.

If she was honest with herself, she would admit that she was disappointed in not seeing Brian tonight. He had a way of quieting her mind after a stressful day. She would instantly relax as soon as his arms went around her. But in her logical mind, she believed she was relieved he wasn't coming, as the conflict in her mind was beginning to overwhelm her. It was at the point where if she thought about her situation for too long, she'd begin to hear a
104

buzzing in her ears. She would have to distract herself by playing with Jasper or putting music on.

As she began to straighten up the store, Claire's words started going through her mind. While no relationship was ever perfect, she tried to figure out what Claire meant when she said the red flags with Ethan were always there. Sure, there were things that had bothered her in the relationship, but that was true of all relationships. She couldn't think of anything that qualified as a red flag.

Once she had cleaned up the remnants of her decorating, she looked over the register receipts on her desk and put it in the folder for tomorrow's paperwork. Feeling drained, she turned off the lights in her office and the back room.

As she was heading to the front, her phone began to ring. She turned it over in her hand and stopped in her tracks when she saw the name. Ethan. She stared at her phone, unmoving, her thumb hovered over the green circle. She wanted to answer it, but at the same time she was afraid to. For reasons unknown to her, she put her phone into her pocket and let it go to voicemail. She locked up the store and went home to take care of her dog.

After she'd taken care of Jasper and the house, she curled up on the sofa in her pajamas, a cup of tea on the table beside her. She grabbed the blanket from the back and snuggled into it. Jasper jumped up and put his head in her lap. Opening her phone, she once again looked at the red circle informing her she had a voicemail. She'd looked at it several times since she got home, but kept putting her phone down without listening to it.

"Well, boy," she said, patting Jasper's head, "let's hear what he has to say." She tapped her phone and put it on speaker.

Hey, Isabella, it's Ethan. I was hoping to talk to you. It's been a while, I know it's my fault and I'm so sorry. Listen . . . . well, I guess the first thing I should tell you is that I moved to New York about six months ago. The city is great. I think you'd love it. Really. But that's not why I'm calling. I, well, the text I sent you. You didn't answer, that's not really like you. . .hope you're okay. . . But, I guess I just wanted to say it's true. I've been thinking about you a lot lately and I miss you.

There was silence for several seconds and Izzy wondered if that was it, but then she heard him continue.

So, I was wondering if you'd like to come down and visit one weekend. Or I could drive up and visit the old hometown . . . but . . . I'd rather you come here. I could show you Central Park, take you to a show. I really do think you'd like it. Anyway, call me back, let me know what you think. I hope you consider it, Izzy. It would be great to see you. And. . .yeah. . .I've really missed you. I hope you believe that.

The voicemail ended. Izzy sat in silence for a while, staring at nothing. She didn't know what she was expecting, but she knew she was not expecting an invitation to visit him. He missed her, he wanted to see her, he wanted to do things with her. Her mind was trying to sort it out, but the buzzing in her ears started again.

Trying to shake it off, she got up, went to the kitchen and grabbed a glass of water. As she was drinking it, she realized there was a knot in her stomach and she felt a little nervous. The buzzing had not subsided. She had no idea what she was going to do.

She hadn't answered his text and she hadn't picked up his call. The one thing she decided was that she didn't want to be rude. She felt he deserved some type of answer, even if it was generic. She grabbed her phone and typed a short text.

Sorry I haven't responded. I got your voicemail.
Let me think about it.

Sighing, she immediately felt guilty. How could she even think about it when she had Brian? Brian made her happy, why was she so confused about this? The buzzing in her head seemed to get louder.

Grabbing the bottle of aspirin she kept on the windowsill above the sink, she opened the lid and shook two out. Looking down at Jasper she asked, "Now what am I going to do?"

EIGHT

After Claire and Greg listened to the voicemail, Izzy clicked off her phone and anxiously awaited their reactions. She hardly slept the night before, consumed by the paradox of Ethan wanting to see her and her growing relationship with Brian. None of the paperwork had gotten done and she had Liza put in extra time at the register. She dodged Brian's phone call and texted him to say she was stopping by Claire's right after work.

Having told Claire about the voicemail earlier in the day, she was eager to hear their thoughts now that they had listened to it. As the message ended, she noticed that her friends exchanged a meaningful glance and couldn't help asking, "Well? Why the look?"

"Well," Claire replied, "we were talking before you got here and it's just a little. . ." She seemed to be looking for the right word.

"It's suspicious," Greg filled in.

"Suspicious? What do you mean?" Izzy looked from Greg to Claire.

"Honey, look at the timing. Isn't it strange that Ethan, who hasn't contacted you in

109

months, suddenly sends a text after you start dating Brian? Saying that he misses you when he hadn't said that for how long? And now this?"

"But that would mean he'd have to know about Brian. For him to know, he'd still have to have a connection to someone in town. As far as I know, he's distanced himself from everyone since he left."

"As far as you know," Greg repeated her words. "We think he might be. The timing is too much of a coincidence. Something just seems off about it."

"Or maybe it could genuinely be a coincidence," Izzy said. "I mean, is it so hard to believe that he really does miss me? There was a time when he loved me. It's not far-fetched to think that he might miss me."

"It's not," Claire answered. "I'm sure he did. We want you to look at this logically, Izzy. Why now? He barely got in touch with you this last year. There was silence for months. You start seeing Brian and this happens. I don't think it's a coincidence. I'm sorry, I don't. I think he knows about Brian and that's why he's texting and calling again."

"There's something else," Greg said, furrowing his eyebrows and looking thoughtful.

110

"Izzy, there's something you haven't touched on yet. There's a detail you've overlooking in this conversation."

"What's that?" Izzy asked.

"When he left town, he moved to Houston, a place you'd have to fly to if you wanted to visit, not that he ever invited you down there," Greg pointed out. "Yet in his call to you, he says he's moved to New York. For six months he doesn't inform you that he's moved and that he's relatively close, just a drive down I-95."

"Until she starts seeing Brian," Claire finished.

Izzy shook her head in disbelief. "You guys want me to believe that the only reason he's reaching out to me is because he heard I'm seeing someone. He's only saying he misses me because he somehow learned about Brian. Are you really implying that he's got a spy here? Someone that is informing him of everything I'm doing?"

"We're not saying he has a spy, Izzy. We're saying he might be keeping in touch with someone who may have told him about Brian." Claire shrugged. "It's possible. It's also logical. It would explain the timing. What it doesn't explain is why he didn't tell you about New York."

"There could be several reasons why he didn't say anything." Even as Izzy said the words, she knew it was odd that he hadn't. She changed direction. "So, let's say you're right that he knows about Brian," Izzy reasoned, "except for this – if he truly did not miss me or had no desire to reconnect, then my involvement with Brian would have no effect on him, right? He could have easily carried on with minimal or even zero communication."

Greg exchanged a knowing glance with Claire. After a moment, Claire spoke, clearing her throat before saying, "Like I told you yesterday when I was at the store, I think you tend to romanticize things when it comes to Ethan."

"Please don't tell me how to remember my own relationship, Claire," Izzy retorted. "I'm the one that lived it. I remember everything."

"Fair enough," Greg said. "Izzy, do you really want to see Ethan? Do you really want to go to New York?"

Claire interjected, "I think what you really need to ask yourself is this; is seeing Ethan worth giving up Brian? A man who is *here*, who is making *permanent* plans?"

"I don't know!" Izzy almost shouted. Then she sighed, and shook her head. "I have been so confused since he sent the text. I keep going back and forth."

Claire's voice was quiet, "Don't do it, Izzy. I know you're confused, but I don't think it's about Brian and Ethan. I think there's something else that frightens you."

"I'm not frightened, Claire. I'm confused." Izzy paused and then looked at her friends. "What's funny is that both Brian and Ethan promised me they would be with me forever. Then they both left. I can't be angry at Brian, I mean we were way too young. I can't be angry at Ethan, either. He was right to pursue his dreams. It was me that didn't want to leave."

There was silence for a few moments before Claire said, "Think about what you just said, Izzy. There's a clue to figuring this out in there."

"What? That I shouldn't be angry with either of them? I'm not. I guess I'm the one I should be angry with. Maybe I'm the one that screwed up somewhere along the way." Izzy sighed again. "All I know is that I think, maybe, I owe it to Ethan to hear him out, to see what's going on in his head, find out what he really wants."

Greg replied, "Do you really think that's the best thing? I'm asking you again, do you really want to visit him?"

"I don't understand why neither of you are getting this. You both know Ethan."

"Yes, we do," Claire said, "and we remember how it was between you two."

"If you tell me one more time that I'm romanticizing it, I'm going to scream."

"Okay," Greg said evenly. "you said you remember everything. Then just take some time to really think about this, Izzy. Really think it over before you do anything. You're overlooking the fact that he's been very close for six months and never told you."

Izzy shifted her gaze between Greg and Claire. She wasn't sure what she had been expecting to hear, but she felt a surge of irritation toward them. She struggled to grasp why they were adamant about Ethan's motives and so dismissive of the possibility that his call was driven by genuine feelings of missing her, rather than calculated timing based on someone informing him of Brian. To her, the idea that it was purely coincidental carried just as much weight, if not more. On top of that, they both apparently thought there was something wrong with her, that she didn't remember things right and she's frightened of something - though of what, she had no clue.

"Okay, got it," she said, standing up and pulling her coat on. "I need to head out. I have Jasper and Brian's coming over." She started walking toward the front door.

"You're going to have to tell Brian about this," Claire said.

Izzy turned around and paused for a second. "I know, Claire. I'm not going to hide anything from him. He deserves nothing less than honesty. He's a good man." She paused again, her shoulders dropped slightly as she fought back the water that was beginning to fill her eyes. "He's a really good man."

"Yes, he is," Greg agreed.

Out on the sidewalk, Izzy pulled on her gloves and turned in the direction of her home. It was beginning to flurry and it felt like the temperature had dropped. As she began walking, her thoughts turned to Brian. Telling him about Ethan's call was the last thing she wanted to do, but she knew she had to. It was important to her to be honest with Brian. The only reason she hadn't talked to him about her late-night thoughts was because she had attributed it to the healing they both said they had to do.

At that moment, she realized she may have been rationalizing that and she let out a sigh. Maybe she should have told him she was struggling. She knew he would have understood. "I'm a mess," she said out loud to no one.

Brian seemed to know her better than she knew herself, she thought. He remembered so many little things from their previous time together that most men would have forgotten, or never even registered in the first place. Izzy always felt lighter, more in tune when she was with him.

With Ethan, she had felt loved and protected. She believed that relationship was going to last forever. There was no imagining life without him. That was until the day he told her he no longer wanted to stay in Willow's End.

What was she supposed to do? If she stayed with Brian, she knew she would be happy, but she would always wonder if there had been a chance with Ethan. Or she could take that chance, find out if there was still something there with Ethan and maybe it would work. Or maybe she'd discover it was Brian she was meant to be with but it would be too late.

No closer to sorting out the mess in her mind than she was before seeing Claire and

Greg, Izzy became heartsick over the thought of what she was about to tell Brian. She was hoping he would understand how confused she was, but knew in her heart he would be hurt. She was risking the relationship with him. She could no longer think straight and the buzzing sound in her head had returned.

Shaking her head, she thought she might need to see a doctor. The buzzing would sometimes lead to a headache. She began to wonder if she was becoming prone to migraines. That was all she needed right now, she thought, as she tried to shift her mind away from what she was going to have to do once she saw Brian.

She was a little over halfway to her house when she noticed a police cruiser pull up alongside her. Glancing over, she saw it was Tim Walker. She gave him a small wave as the car pulled to a stop.

Putting the window down, Tim called, "Hey, Izzy. Heading home?" She nodded. "You know the snow is going to pick up. You want a lift?" Izzy nodded again, walked over and got into the car.

"Thanks, Tim," she said as they pulled away from the curb. "I appreciate it."

"No problem. I'm here to serve, my lady." He let out a chuckle. "Anyway, there's a

117

storm coming up the corridor. Pennsylvania, New Jersey, New York, they're all getting rain. We're gonna get snow. Weather Channel says about 6 to 8 inches, so not a big one, just enough to be a pain. The guys should have it all plowed by lunch tomorrow."

"I forgot about the snow coming," Izzy answered. "I saw it on my phone last night, but I was too. . .distracted. . .today. Forgot all about it. You should have a very quiet night, then."

"I should," Tim answered. "But you know, there's always that one idiot that forgets to open the flue in their chimney before they start a fire. Smoke alarms go off, they panic, call us or the fire department."

"Didn't Charlie do that last year?" Izzy laughed.

Tim nodded. "Thought Barb was going to knock him out right there in the street. It was funny. She's out there in her robe and slippers screaming at the poor guy. Although, she wasn't wrong, if I'm being honest."

Making her laugh with other stories of winter mishaps, Tim had taken her mind off her predicament for a few minutes. When he turned onto her street and then into her driveway, it came flooding back to her and she fell silent.

She took a deep breath, reached for the door handle and thanked Tim again for the ride.

"You okay, Izzy?" Tim asked.

Izzy smiled. "Yes, it's been a very long day, that's all." She got out of the car.

"Give Brian my best," Tim said as he gave her a wave.

"Will do," she replied before shutting the door. She turned toward the house, the heaviness of the impending discussion weighing on her mind. As she ascended the steps, mixed emotions tugged at her heart. The anticipation of seeing Brian was coupled with a sense of dread. The conflicting desire to be with him clashed with the discomfort of what she needed to tell him, creating a discordant inner turmoil. If only she could rewind time, finding solace in the simplicity of when it was only her and Jasper, away from the complexity of the situation she currently found herself in.

Jasper greeted her as soon as she opened the door. Sinking down to his level, she scratched his ears and confided, "You know, my big boy, maybe you're the only man I need in my life."

If He Comes Back

NINE

"Wow," Brian lowered his eyes and clasped his hands together. Sitting on the sofa after Izzy had conveyed both the phone call and the struggle she'd been having, it was clear Brian hadn't been prepared for what he'd just heard.

Izzy didn't know what to say. A knot formed in her stomach, and she began to wish she hadn't told him. The look in his eyes was killing her. She wanted to take the words back. Hurting him was the last thing she had wanted to do, but she knew she had to be honest with him. Letting him process what she'd told him, she sat quietly, waiting for him to speak again.

It seemed like hours, but it had been only a few minutes before Brian turned to her. "What are you going to do?"

"I don't know," Izzy replied. It was an honest answer. She hadn't called Ethan back yet, and she wasn't going to until she knew what she was going to do.

Brian nodded, sat back and ran his hand through his hair. He let out a long sigh and looked at her again. "Look, Iz, I'd be lying if I said I understood. Truth is, I don't. I don't believe this." Brian's voice began to rise. "What the hell, Izzy? The guy left three years ago, hasn't come back, barely talked to you for months, and you're thinking about what? Talking to him again? Going down there?"

"I don't know. I know how this looks," Izzy answered. "Maybe. . ." She trailed off, not sure of what she wanted to say. It was true she didn't know why she was considering it. At first she thought it was because she had to find out if he still had feelings for her, but then she thought of Claire's words and confusion set in. If he did still have feelings for her, he would have let her know long before now. He would have called instead of letting the communication dwindle - but then she would think there had to be a reason for that, and maybe that's what she needed to find out. The buzzing in her head started again.

"I thought things with us were going. . .were heading. . .I thought it was good, Iz. I thought this was what we both wanted." Brian said quietly. Izzy could hear the hurt in his voice.

"I did. I do," she paused. "I'm just so confused. I hope you can try to understand how difficult this is. I cherish every minute we've spent together. When you and I started spending time together I didn't think I'd ever talk to or see Ethan again. He contacted me and there's a part of me that. . . I don't know. . .needs answers, I guess."

"He knew how you felt, Izzy," Brian voice had an angry edge to it. He shook his head. "That should be your answer. He knew. And he left, anyway."

"So did you, Brian. You left, too." The words came out of nowhere and surprised Izzy. She brought her hand up to her mouth. Seeing the look on Brian's face, she whispered through her fingers, "I'm sorry. That wasn't fair."

Brian stood up and walked over to the chair to get his coat. He turned to Izzy. "I was going to college. We both decided the long-distance thing wasn't working. And then you wouldn't . . .you said. . ." He stopped. He shook his head again as he put his coat on. "Not even close to being the same thing, Iz. Not even close."

Moving toward the door, he paused and faced her with a weary expression. "I refuse to be your second choice, Izzy. I won't settle for being a backup plan." With a resigned shake of his head, he reached for the door handle.

"Brian, wait," Izzy called, her voice trembling and tears welling up in her eyes. As she stood up, the weight of the situation settled heavily on her shoulders, she took a step toward him. Just as she reached out to him, her phone began to ring and it stopped her.

Their gazes both shifted to the coffee table as the phone illuminated and displayed the caller's name. Izzy and Brian exchanged a quick but loaded glance before looking back at the phone. Izzy turned to Brian again, but he avoided her eyes, opting instead to pull his gloves from his pocket and put them on.

"Answer it," he said in a curt tone before turning and walking out the door.

Izzy took a tentative step toward the door, her heart heavy with the war of emotions going on inside her. As the tears spilled down her cheeks, she felt a mix of sadness and uncertainty wash over her. The persistent ringing of the phone filled the air, a stark reminder of the reality she was facing. With a trembling hand, she reached out and grabbed the phone, her fingers fumbling as she wiped away the tears that blurred her vision.

"Ethan," she answered, her voice caught between emotions.

"Hey, Izzy! I got your text. I was hoping you'd call back last night with an answer."

Izzy's mind raced, a whirlwind of thoughts and emotions colliding within her. Her gaze lingered on the door like a silent plea for answers that seemed out of reach. She felt her shoulders slump under the weight, fresh tears welling in her eyes. Turning from the door, she searched for words and struggled to make sense of the feelings and of the thoughts running through her mind.

Her hand instinctively rose to the top of her head as she shut her eyes, trying to stop the chaos her mind had become. She tried to gather her thoughts and push down the emotions.

"Isabella?" Ethan's voice made her eyes snap open.

"Why didn't you tell me you moved to New York?" Izzy hadn't planned on making that the first thing she said to him, but it was the first thing that came out.

A heavy silence lingered on the other end of the line, punctuated only by the distant hum of street noise filtering through. Izzy wondered where he was – was he in an office, a restaurant, or perhaps his apartment? Memories of their past conversations flooded her mind, vivid images of his office in Houston and his cozy apartment there flashed through.

However, at that moment, reality hit her like a wave. Where once she had known his surroundings, as she had often seen them when they would video chat, she now knew nothing of where he worked or where he lived. She had no idea what his life was even remotely like anymore.

A few more seconds passed before Ethan answered. "I guess . . .I don't know. I think I just wanted to make sure I got myself established here first."

"You could have told me. So, are you established now?"

"It's going well," Ethan answered. "But, look, I really want you to come down. I really want to see you, and I think you'll like the city. I could show you around."

"I've seen it," came Izzy's answer.

"You have?" Ethan sounded surprised.

"I'm not a recluse, Ethan. Claire and I have been there a few times the last two years. I've seen Central Park, I've seen the Museum of Modern Art, the Guggenheim. I've been to a couple Broadway shows. I even walked across the Brooklyn Bridge."

"Then you've seen how great it is. There's still a lot for you to see." He paused. "I can't believe you've been here."

Izzy let out a weary sigh, "Well, it's not like we've talked a lot lately," she murmured
126

softly. When Ethan didn't respond, she felt a sense of unease in the silence. Pushing back against the uncertainty, Izzy asked another question she hadn't planned on. "Why now, Ethan?"

When Ethan asked what she meant, Izzy found it only served to stir frustration within her. It wasn't a question she thought she needed to spell out for him. She thought it was pretty self-explanatory.

"You haven't mentioned missing me in a long time. You've been in New York for months now, not that far away. You could have made the effort to see me or even just pick up the phone. You didn't." A tinge of hurt and confusion colored her words. There was once a time she had wanted nothing more than to reconnect with Ethan and now, here he was. But so was Brian. The turmoil was creating a divide in her mind and her emotions.

She repeated her question. "Why now?"

Izzy heard the deep sigh. It was followed by silence. A silence she wasn't going to break. When she used to envision talking to Ethan again, this wasn't how she had seen it going. For a split second she wondered if she was being too hard on him, but then realized it was a simple question. She waited for him to answer.

"I told you," Ethan finally replied. "I didn't want you to come until I got myself in a good place here. I didn't want you here when I was living in a one room hole in the wall and getting set up. I know you. You would have taken one look at it and tried to convince me to go back to Willow's End. Is it wrong that I wanted to get myself settled before asking the person that means the most to me to come down and see it?"

Izzy didn't immediately respond. She had been thrown by the words 'person that means the most to me'. Beginning to soften, she murmured, "I guess not."

"Look, I know I should have stayed in touch. I'm an idiot. I don't have an excuse, but you have to know I thought about you every day. You know that. I didn't tell you I missed you because, well, you know I do. How could I not?"

Rubbing her temple, the buzzing in her head increased and it was beginning to hurt. She took in his words but couldn't focus on them. "Ethan, I'm sorry. It's been a long day, and I'm getting a headache."

"But, Izzy, I really want you to come down. Will you think about it?"

"Okay, yes," Izzy said, the buzzing getting louder. "I'll think about it. I'll call you when I make up my mind. I really have to go. Good night, Ethan."

"Bye, Isabella."

Izzy ended the call, set her phone on the coffee table and sunk into the sofa. She put her hands up to her face and inhaled. Try as she might, the burn behind her eyelids told her the tears weren't going to stay in. She sat there, crying into her hands. The chaos, the frustration, the conflicted thoughts and emotions, all came tumbling out.

After a few minutes, Jasper jumped on the sofa and nudged her hands. Taking them away from her face, she began to pet him. Pulling him close to her, she gave him a tight hug. Then she straightened up, and glanced at the door.

Picking up her phone she took a chance and sent a text.

I'm so sorry. I needed to be honest with you. Can we please talk?

She waited. She could see the text was read almost immediately after she sent it. Five minutes passed, then ten, then twenty. She knew she couldn't blame him if he didn't reply. Getting up, she slowly turned the lights off, let Jasper out, straightened up the kitchen and then made her way upstairs.

Guilt overtook her. She sat on the edge of her bed and once again let the tears come. She didn't understand herself anymore. *What are you doing?* she asked herself. She began to ask herself questions, none of which she had an answer to. Did she just destroy her relationship with Brian? Would he answer her text? Would he talk to her? What if she just killed the relationship she really wanted? Did Ethan really miss her? If he does, then does he want her back? What if she saw Ethan and realized it was a mistake? What if it wasn't?

Her head began to ache again, as the incessant buzzing wouldn't stop. She got up to get some aspirin when she heard her phone ding. She stopped and hesitated, afraid that it was Brian and of what he might say. She picked it up.

Are you going?

She sat back down and typed out a reply, deleted it, typed a few more, deleted those and then finally sent one.

I am so very confused. I don't know.

Then what is there to say?

I didn't mean for this to happen.

I know.

Izzy wasn't sure what to say. She thought about ending the texts and calling him. Her heart was aching at the thought that she may have lost Brian as both a boyfriend and a friend. She was about to call when another text came in.

Maybe we jumped into this too fast. We said we'd take it slow but maybe we shouldn't have gotten into whatever this was right away. I think we should just do what we gotta do.

Are you ending things?

Do you expect me to stay when you're thinking about going off to someone else?

I didn't say I'm going. I don't even know what I'm thinking right now. All I know is you mean so much to me and I'm so sorry that I hurt you.

Do what you gotta do.

I don't know what that is.

I'm really sorry to hear that. Goodnight, Izzy.

Setting down her phone, Izzy went numb. She knew she shouldn't be upset or angry with Brian. But knowing she brought it on herself didn't ease anything. She felt emotionally drained and suddenly, she was beyond tired. The sleepless nights she'd been having in addition to the headaches and emotional rollercoaster she'd been on caught up to her. She crawled under the covers and curled up in a ball. Silent tears began falling onto her pillow.

TEN

It turned out that, for Izzy, emotional turmoil served as the best cure for insomnia. Even though she was still tired, she hadn't tossed and turned until the wee hours of the morning, as she had been the last few nights. Her mind seemed to be a bit clearer and she took on a logical approach to her problem.

She knew it wasn't a good idea to reach out to Brian right away, not after their texts last night, so she focused on Ethan. After going over her conversation with Ethan several times in her mind, she felt she had made sense of it.

She checked her phone several times during the morning. Though she wouldn't blame Brian if he didn't text or call her, it seemed as if a part of her still held out hope. She thought maybe she might hear something from him. By noon, she was fairly certain she wouldn't hear from him again for quite a while. There was a part of her that began to be upset that he couldn't understand how conflicted she was.

The morning had been spent restocking shelves and redoing the Christmas display, all while trying to logically think things through.

By the time she met Claire for lunch, she thought she had it all worked out.

"So, he ended it," Claire said, after listening to Izzy relay the events of the previous night.

"He left," Izzy replied. "I tried to get him to understand how messed up my mind is but he left."

Claire's eyes opened wide. "You gave him no choice, Izzy. Please name one man who would sit around and wait for a girl to *maybe* choose him after she's gone to visit her former boyfriend to see if anything is still there. You pushed him away."

"I was being honest with him," Izzy began to feel angry. "You know, just like you said I would have to be."

Sighing, Claire said, "Of course you had to be honest. That fact that you are even entertaining the thought of going to see Ethan is what pushed him away. Jesus, Izzy."

"I know he had a reason, Claire. It's only, you know, Brian used to know me so well. But now he couldn't see how confused I was. He couldn't understand how anyone would be confused by this. So, instead of trying to understand it, he left."

Claire sat back in her chair and stared at Izzy for a few moments. "Is that what you're telling yourself? You still don't see it, do you?"

"See what?" Izzy asked.

Claire shook her head. "Well, it really doesn't matter now, but I'm going to be honest with you. You've got a major issue you have not dealt with. You–"

Izzy didn't let her finish. "Oh, my God! Stop telling me I have issues. Yeah, I do. I've been completely blindsided by not one - but two - exes coming back into my life and I don't understand how people can't see that would confuse the hell out of anyone."

"Relax," Claire replied. "Of course we know that can be confusing."

"Okay, then," Izzy said. "I thought about it a lot this morning and I think I've worked this out."

Claire was silent throughout Izzy's long-winded and, in Claire's opinion, sugar-coated explanation of why she was considering visiting Ethan in New York. Izzy noticed, but kept on rambling instead of asking for Claire's thoughts since she already knew them. She wasn't even sure why she'd asked to go to lunch when she knew what Claire would say.

Finally, Claire set down her fork and looked at Izzy. Her face was a mask of stone. "I'm not doing this anymore, Izzy." She held up her hands. "You've hurt Brian. No, you intentionally sabotaged your relationship with him and now you're rationalizing why you might go to New York. Do what you want. You're going to anyway, but I really don't want to hear about it anymore."

Before Izzy could reply, Brooke walked up to the table and greeted them. "Hey, guys, just wanted to stop by and say hi. I'm picking lunch up for the boss." She held up the take-out bag she was holding.

"I'm surprised it's not a bigger bag," Claire laughed, changing demeanor.

"Ren says he's on a diet," Brooke answered and then turned to Izzy. "We should have a girls night again, all of us together. Those were some fun nights."

Izzy nodded, "We should."

"We might be long overdue for one," Claire said. "Though, unlike last time, we'll need to stay away from the beach. I just might throw Izzy into the ocean."

"She's kidding," Izzy said when she saw Brooke's face.

Brooke nodded, "Okay then, call me whenever you want to have one. Gotta run." Brooke turned and made her way out.

"No, I wasn't," Claire said, but Izzy didn't reply.

Silence fell over the table. Izzy pushed the remaining food around the plate with her fork. After a few minutes she looked up at Claire. "Look–"

"No," Claire cut her off. "I mean it, Izzy. It's true what they say - you can lead a horse to water, but you can't make him drink. This is the last time I'm going to ask you this."

"Ask me what?"

"What are you so afraid of?"

Izzy let out an exasperated breath. "Nothing, Claire. I don't know why you ask me that. If I was afraid, I wouldn't be thinking about visiting New York."

"New York?" Tim asked, as he came up to the table. "What about it?"

Izzy replied, "Nothing."

Tim looked back and forth between the girls, shrugged and changed subjects. "If you ladies haven't already seen the forecast, a big storm might be hitting us this weekend." He let out a long breath. "They're keeping an eye on it and it may change course, but they're saying, as of now, we might be looking at a foot or more."

"I'll believe it when I see it," Claire said. "Forecasts aren't always accurate that far out."

"Well, it's Monday and they're saying it's gonna hit Friday, so we'll see. Like I said, it may change course, but we don't get that lucky."

"At least we'll have a white Christmas," Izzy answered.

"If we do get it, what will that mean for Carol and Frank's Christmas party at the inn?" Claire asked. "They spend so much time on it. It's a tradition to kick off the Christmas season at the inn. It would be a shame if they have to cancel."

"It's not supposed to start until late Friday night. I don't think they'd cancel, even if it starts early. Everyone looks forward to it. I think people would walk through a foot of snow to get there."

"You're probably right," Claire replied.

"Anyway, I'm just making sure everyone is prepared."

"And have their flue open?" Izzy laughed.

Tim chuckled. "Yes, definitely. Enjoy the rest of your lunch, ladies. I'm gonna have a few words with Charlie before I hit the street again." He turned and headed toward the bar.

"Hit the street," Claire murmured and shook her head. "Like we have a lot of crime here. He's lucky if they get a drunk and disorderly once a month."

Izzy nodded and continued eating, hesitant to go back to the conversation they were having. Her mind wasn't as jumbled as it had been the night before. She was beginning to think there was no harm in going down for a weekend and finding out what Ethan was thinking, and how he was feeling about her. After all, she thought, it would be better all the way around if she knew, so she could get on with her life one way or the other.

She noticed Claire hadn't picked up their conversation, either. Claire seemed intent on finishing her lunch in a hurry. It was unusual for them to sit in silence. Izzy could hear bits of conversation from other people's tables. She thought she heard someone mention Ethan and her ears pricked up. She lifted her eyes and glanced across the table, but Claire didn't appear to have heard it.

Lifting her head, Izzy looked toward the bar and saw Tim and Charlie talking. She thought it sounded like a male voice who had uttered the words. Her eyes swept the room, but there were only a handful of people at the tables, and most of them were female. Maybe she'd just imagined it, she thought. She tried to hear what Tim and Charlie were saying, but she couldn't pick anything up clearly.

"I know you're probably gonna go." Claire's voice startled Izzy and she turned back to her friend. "I'm not going to pretend I'm happy about this. I'm not. You know that." Claire sighed and paused for a few moments. "But, whatever decision you make, I'll still love you. I meant it when I said I don't want to talk about it anymore, though. I may not like the decision you end up making, I may not support it, but I'll support *you* and I'll still love you."

"Thank you, Claire," Izzy replied and reached for her hand. "That means so much. I love you."

"I know. Everybody does," Claire laughed.

Izzy released Claire's hand and clasped her own under her chin. She looked at Claire for a few seconds and then said, "I feel like I have to go. I think." Claire didn't respond, and Izzy felt there was really nothing else left to say.

After finishing lunch and heading to the store, Izzy was in her office going over the finances. Her mind kept drifting back to Brian. They had been taking it slow, and she had loved every minute she spent with him. Still, she felt she needed to see Ethan to either get answers or put the relationship in the rearview mirror once and for all.

The image of Brian walking out of her house the night before kept flashing through her mind. Each time it did, she felt her eyes begin to water. She wanted to talk to him, but what would she say? There wasn't anything she could say that would make him feel better.

She found herself second-guessing herself again. Thinking about Claire's words from a few days ago, was going to see Ethan worth this? She'd been almost certain this morning that she should go, but now she was beginning to think it wasn't worth it and she wanted to call Brian and tell him she'd been wrong. Then her mind went back to Ethan.

Letting out a frustrated grunt, she tried to refocus on the paperwork in front of her. Izzy was pleased to see that sales were up over last year. She wasn't surprised as the economy was doing better and people were beginning to spend money again. Her thoughts were interrupted again when she heard her name being called from the floor.

As she walked out front, she saw Carol standing by the counter. She went to the horror section and grabbed a copy of Stephen King's latest off the shelf.

"Hi, Carol," Izzy greeted the older woman. "Here you go, as promised."

"Wonderful!" Carol replied as Izzy gave the book to Liza to ring up. "I can't wait to start this one!"

"I hope the forecast isn't scaring you out of canceling the party Friday," Izzy commented.

Carol waved her hand as if brushing it away. "Oh, not at all. It'll go on as it does every year. People who live outside of town might decide not to come, but I've heard from so many people they'd show up no matter what. Brian said he'd clear off the snow if it starts during the party. He's such a good boy." Carol stopped and laughed at herself. "Listen to me, he's certainly not a boy anymore!"

Izzy smiled but didn't say anything. The realization that she wouldn't be at the party with Brian seeped into her brain. He still hadn't texted or called, and after the way he left last night, she wasn't sure if she'd hear from him at all. She knew she would have to reach out first, but she already knew there was nothing she could say to make him understand.

"I don't know how he does it," Carol was still talking. "He's fixing up his father's house, working full-time, he helped us with the Wi-Fi and even installed new programs for the inn's bookkeeping. It makes everything so much easier."

"He sounds like a great guy to have around," Liza chimed in. Izzy knew Liza was smiling in her direction but kept her eyes focused on Carol since she hadn't told Liza it was over.

"He is," Carol continued. "I just worry he's taking on too much. On top of his father's house, he's gonna go and buy that old factory building, though what he plans on doing with it I don't know." Carol paused and then her eyes widened. "I wasn't supposed to tell anyone that. Oh, girls, please keep that to yourselves, won't you?"

"Of course, Carol, don't worry," Liza said from behind the register.

Izzy wasn't sure if she'd heard correctly. Surely, Carol didn't mean Brian was going to

143

buy the old shoe factory. He wouldn't have kept that from her. That's a secret that wouldn't be kept for too long in this town, regardless of who was told to keep it to themselves.

"You don't mean the old shoe factory, do you?" When Izzy saw Carol nod, she continued, "Are you sure it was Brian that's going to buy it?"

Carol nodded again. "I wasn't supposed to tell anyone. He was so excited about it, and he's going to be so upset with me. I ruined the surprise. Izzy, please don't tell him I let it slip."

"Of course, I won't," Izzy answered, her mind trying to process the information she just received.

After Carol left, Izzy went back to her office. Unfinished paperwork in front of her, and her computer screen blinking at her, she ignored them both. She kept going over what Carol had said, especially the comment about ruining the surprise. In her heart, she knew what the surprise was supposed to be, though her mind was refusing to accept it.

Her computer screen kept blinking at her, but she continued to stare into space. Buying the factory was such a huge investment that she couldn't imagine he would keep it from her. Yet, he had. She wondered who else besides Marty and the Bowens knew about it. Had he told any of them what his plan for it was? Her mind went through several reasons why he could have bought it, but she kept coming back to the same one.

Had Brian bought the factory so they could put into action their long-ago dream?

If He Comes Back

ELEVEN

Several days later, juggling boxes while controlling Jasper on his leash, Izzy was nearing the post office when she almost crashed right into Brooke. The top box slid off and fell to the sidewalk.

"Oh, my God, I'm so sorry," Izzy said as she set the other box down.

"Don't worry about it," Brooke replied. "You didn't run into me. It's all good. Here, let me help you with that." Brooke bent down, stacked the boxes on top of each other and held them out to Izzy. "No harm, no foul, and nothing damaged." She smiled broadly at Izzy.

"Thanks," Izzy answered as she slid her free arm under the boxes and took them.

"Izzy," Brooke said hesitantly, "I ran into Brian last night at Misty's. I don't know what happened, he didn't say. In fact, he hardly talked at all. I'm just going to give you something to think about. Guys like that don't stay on the market long."

Closing her eyes, Izzy let out a breath. Brian wasn't a subject she wanted to talk about with Brooke. She knew Brooke had gone to see him at the inn when he first came back to town. Izzy remembered the jealousy she felt when she'd heard about it. She genuinely liked Brooke, but she felt herself getting irritated. The last thing she needed was to be reminded that other women would love to take Brian off the market.

"I'll keep that in mind," Izzy answered, then tilted her head toward the boxes. "Gotta get these in the mail, Christmas presents for my parents. Have a good day, Brooke."

Continuing on to the post office, the irritation did not subside. She knew she shouldn't feel that way. After all, it was her decision knowing that Brian might walk away from her. Her head had been spinning since she found out he'd bought the factory. She wanted to talk to Claire about it, but Claire had been adamant about not wanting to talk about it anymore, so she didn't call her.

The other thing she didn't do was let Ethan know she'd decided to go to New York. The weekend between Christmas and New Year's Day seemed like a good time. She thought it would be nice to see the city decorated for the holidays, maybe even see the tree at Rockefeller Center. Meaning to call him to let him know, Izzy found herself interrupted or distracted each time.

After dropping the boxes off, Izzy decided to take Jasper for a short walk before taking him home and heading to the store. The factory was on her mind. She wanted to talk to Brian about it, but he still hadn't called or texted her. Plus, she'd given Carol her word that she wouldn't tell anyone. She was almost certain Brian was thinking about buying it with the intention of the two of them working together to create the plan they had so long ago. That must have been what Carol meant when she said the surprise had been ruined. It would also explain why he had been so vague those times he had been late or had canceled lunch. There was a part of her that thought it was an incredibly romantic gesture. She remembered Brian telling her she was a sucker for them, and he was right.

However, the other side of her reasoned that she hadn't asked him to buy it. She also considered the idea that he may not be buying it for that reason. It was a possibility that he had other plans for it; maybe he was going to restore it and flip it, or maybe he planned on making it a hotel. Izzy pondered other reasons he might consider the purchase, but she kept coming back to the plan they had. She thought Brian had been right; it was still a good plan.

She tried to shift her thoughts to Ethan and realized she still hadn't called him. Making a mental note to do it as soon as she got to the store, Izzy was also imagining what New York City must be like at Christmas. She was sure it looked festive and beautiful, but thoughts of all the noise and the crowds of people crept in. It was why she didn't like the city. The idea of Christmastime in the city seemed magical, until the reality of bumper to bumper traffic and people pushing through the streets factored into it.

Izzy came to a stop before crossing the street, and let out a short gasp. She hadn't realized where she had been walking. The factory stood diagonally across the street from where she stood. The large brick building was set back from the street, with the parking lot wrapping around from the front to the back. Looking at the ornate stone carvings over the doors and the tall windows, Izzy was once again reminded of how beautiful architecture had been in the late 19th and early 20th century. There was so much character in these buildings, not like the sterile, "modern" designs of more recent buildings. It was her comment on the beauty of the building that led to her and Brian planning out what they could do with it.

In a town where every corner whispered echoes of their younger selves, it was both a balm and a sting. The memory made her smile, yet knowing that she had hurt him quickly made the smile fade. Brian had told her he wasn't going to be her backup. If she went to see Ethan, and it didn't work out, there was no way she could hope for any kind of reconciliation with Brian. She wouldn't ask that of him, nor would she expect him to come back.

Ethan's absence shaped her, but so had their time together, and the last three years she had believed that the story they had begun together never really ended—it just paused. The rest of the story had yet to be written. If she went to New York, she'd know if they were going to write many more chapters, or write the ending. Either way, she had to unpause the story and find out.

Turning back the way she came, Izzy began walking Jasper home. The store had to be opened, and the paperwork she'd been pushing aside needed to get done. She occupied her mind with a list of things that needed to get done. In addition to the paperwork, she still had Christmas shopping to finish, wrapping to do, laundry, cleaning, and figuring out what she was taking to the party at the inn the following night.

Izzy was looking forward to the party. Carol and Frank always made it a grand, yet homey, event. The decorations were always beautiful with a Victorian Era vibe, the fireplace in the dining hall always roared with a bright fire and a mix of Christmas music and current songs would come through the speakers. Although the guests bring the food, a potluck to an extent, everyone goes all out. Everything is always delicious and people always joke about how much weight they've gained over the course of the evening.

With Jasper dropped off at home, Izzy was sitting at her desk finally getting through the neglected paperwork. She finished the inventory, payroll, and was almost finished with the financials when she heard Liza call her name. Sighing, she got up and walked to the front. There was a long line of people waiting to check out. Izzy walked behind the counter and opened the second register.

"Brian was just in," Liza said as she was ringing up a sale. "He didn't buy anything."

Startled, Izzy asked, "What did he want?" Disappointment washed over her as she realized he had been in the store but hadn't asked to see her.

"He was looking at your paintings again." Liza turned to the customer. "Thank you, Beth. Have a good day." Turning back to Izzy, she continued, "He asked if you were still set on not selling them. I told him you were and then he left. That was it."

Izzy finished with the customer in front of her and welcomed the next one. She recalled her conversation with Brian when he first came back to town. Having explained to him why she wasn't willing to sell her work, she wondered why he'd come back to ask. She was surprised he'd come at all let alone ask about her paintings, especially now.

When the last customer had been checked out, Liza began balancing her register. Izzy walked to the door, flipped the sign to closed, and locked the door. Turning back, she began the task of straightening the shelves. People always seemed to leave them somewhat of a mess. Her pet peeve, though, were the people who put books where they didn't belong; who chose not to buy a book or chose another one and instead of walking it back to where it belonged, they simply put it on the nearest shelf.

"Want me to do your register?" Liza asked.

"Sure. Thank you," Izzy answered, though she was barely paying attention. She had been cleaning up the gift section when her paintings caught her eye. Staring at the painting of Winding Lake with the willow trees, she was filled with memories of Brian - both past and present.

Reaching out, she ran a finger over their willow tree. Once again, she wondered what she was doing. Only a few months ago, it was just her and Jasper. Alone with her dog and her thoughts of Ethan, her life was simpler. Now here she was, conflicted, confused, and, if she were to admit it to herself, sad. She had gotten what she had believed she wanted over the last three years - Ethan wanted to see her. He wanted her to visit him. He was excited to show her his life in New York.

Yet, she missed Brian. She missed the laughter, the conversations, and how easy it was to be with him. Snuggling on the sofa watching a movie, having popcorn fights, taking Jasper for a walk, stealing kisses while she was working - she missed all of it.

Brian had been in the store, though, and had avoided seeing her. Though she understood why he would do that, she had to acknowledge that it stung. The image of him walking out her door went through her mind yet again. The feeling of wanting to talk to him came back, but she quickly reminded herself that there was nothing she could say to him that would make him understand or erase the hurt she had seen in his eyes.

Izzy ran her finger over their willow tree one more time, then turned and finished straightening up the gift section.

Walking back to the counter, Izzy saw Liza staring at her. Without moving her eyes away from Izzy, Liza asked quietly, "Why are you so afraid?"

Izzy furrowed her eyebrows and gave Liza a look that conveyed she did not appreciate the question.

"Never mind," Liza said. "Forget I said anything."

Izzy grabbed the bank bag and retreated into her office. Sitting down, she folded her arms and shook her head. She could not for the life of her understand why both Claire and Liza thought she was afraid of something.

She picked up the phone to call Claire and then set it down again. Claire had made it clear she didn't want to discuss it anymore. Picking up a pencil she began to play with it and she went into deep thought. She no longer felt sane, she decided. Her thoughts were always jumbled, she went back and forth on whether or not she was making the right decision, and even when she thought she was thinking clearly, she would second guess herself.

She put her head on her desk and let out a long sigh. At least she didn't have a headache today, she thought. Therapy was starting to look like a good an viable option.

This wasn't like her. She knew that. Regardless of what Claire, and now Liza, said, she didn't feel as if she was afraid of anything. If she had to put a label on it, she'd say she felt out of control. Her emotions were definitely out of control and she had no idea how to rein them in and make sense out of them.

For a moment, she thought about calling her mother, but realized it wasn't a very good idea. She hadn't told her about Brian or Ethan during their phone conversations. She wasn't even sure why that was. Her mother had liked both of them, she might have been the one to give her an objective point of view. Although, her mother might have leaned more toward Ethan, since he had often schmoozed her over the phone, or in person the two times he'd gone with her to Arizona. Even though her mother had liked Brian, she'd been quite taken with Ethan.

Without anyone she felt she could talk to, she gathered her things and headed out. On the walk home, she tried to clear her mind. More than anything, she wanted to feel sane again. She wanted to feel normal. She wondered how

156

she could let two men make her feel this way. It wasn't them, she decided, it was definitely her.

Why, though? The question went through her head. All she wanted to do was think clearly and make a decision she knew would be the right one. So, why couldn't she get herself together?

If He Comes Back

TWELVE

The inn was as magnificent and charming as it always was for the party. The dining hall took Izzy's breath away as she walked in carrying the lemon tarts she had prepared the night before. She had decided to make a traditional Victorian dessert since Carol and Frank liked to add a touch of the era to their Christmas holidays.

Greeting friends and neighbors on her way to the dessert table, Izzy spotted Claire and Greg near the fireplace. She set the tarts on the table and stopped to get a glass of wine before heading over to talk to her friends.

"Well, don't you two clean up nicely!" Izzy said in greeting.

Claire spun around in her sparkling red dress before replying, "Thank you! I love this dress. I think I'm going to start wearing it everywhere. But, girl, look at you! Gold is your color."

Izzy lowered her head and smiled, "Thank you."

"You look like a couple of Christmas balls standing side by side," Greg said.

Claire's mouth opened wide. "What do you mean by that, exactly? We're not round, dear!"

Izzy couldn't help laughing at the look on Greg's face as he stammered his explanation that it was only their colors and not their shapes. Claire lightly smacked his shoulder and then changed the subject to the work involved in getting ready for the holidays ahead. Commiserating on how much time the decorating took, how much shopping needed to be done yet, along with baking, Izzy and Claire barely noticed Greg's demeanor change until he nudged Claire.

Slightly annoyed, Claire looked at her husband as he lifted his chin in the direction of the doorway. Izzy saw Claire look over. Before Izzy could do the same, Claire took her by the arm and led her to the table of appetizers, claiming to be famished. Izzy tried to turn around, but Claire was suddenly yammering about needing her advice. It was a situation so minor that Izzy interrupted her.

"Stop," she said, "You don't really don't need my advice." Izzy deliberately looked over the hall and saw Brian talking with Carol and Frank. She looked back at Claire. "Really? Was that necessary? Of course he'd be here tonight.

He stayed here when he first got back. I would have been disappointed if he *hadn't* shown."

Claire looked at her friend as if debating whether or not to say something.

"What?" Izzy asked. "Is there something I don't know?"

"Brooke made a play for Brian last night."

Izzy took a moment before replying. "Well, I can't say I'm surprised. I ran into her yesterday morning. She said guys like Brian don't stay on the market long." She looked back at Brian, still with Carol and Frank, smiling and enjoying the conversation. Turning back to Claire, she asked, "How do you know she made a play for him?"

"We were at Misty's and we saw it happen – or start to happen, I should say. She started flirting, he didn't seem interested. But they did end up talking for a while. I wanted get in between them but Greg stopped me. He told me not to meddle."

Nodding, Izzy felt a knot in her stomach. She knew she didn't have a right to feel jealous. He'd made it clear he wasn't going to be any kind of backup. If things didn't work out with Ethan and they got back together, he would always feel he was with her by default. She could never do that to him, she would never ask that of him. He was too good of a man.

Looking at Claire, Izzy said, "He has every right to talk to whoever he wants to."

"That's not how you really feel, Izzy. I can see it in your eyes," Claire replied.

"It's true, though. When I told him about Ethan, he said he wasn't going to be my backup and he left. It was valid for him to do that. He's a wonderful man and he doesn't deserve to ever feel like he's someone's second choice." She heard her words and knew them to be true, but she couldn't help her eyes from starting to well up.

"Is he really second choice?" Claire asked. "Look at you, Izzy. Is he really second?"

Izzy shook her head and said, "I really don't want to talk about it."

Claire sighed. "So, when are you going to New York?"

"Between Christmas and New Year's," Izzy replied and then realized she had forgotten, again, to call Ethan. The store was busy, and then she made the tarts as soon as she had gotten home. Today was just as busy between the store and getting ready for the party.

She shook her head. "I don't know what's going on with me. First, every now and then I get this buzzing in my ears, I can't focus on anything and I'm forgetting more than I remember."

"It's not hard to figure out what's wrong, Izzy," Claire said. "I don't think it takes a rocket scientist. You've decided to go to New York, but do you really want to go?"

"That's what I mean, Claire. Yes. I've thought it over. I've gone over it in my mind a lot, and, yes, I think I need to go. I think. But, I forgot to call Ethan and let him know I'm coming. Things just became so busy, but I've also let other things slide and my mind is all over the road. I don't know which end is up anymore. I think I may go into therapy."

"Maybe you should. I think it's a good idea. But Izzy, objectively, you can't draw any conclusions as to why you're feeling like this?" Claire asked.

Izzy made an attempt at a joke, alluding to an old song. "Maybe I should just visit the Tallahatchie Bridge."

"Want me to drive you to Mississippi?" Claire didn't miss a beat.

"Seriously, though, I've made up my mind. I know you don't like it, but I think that - maybe - I owe it to myself to get answers, one way or the other. I think."

"If that's your choice, then you're right. Brian can talk to whoever he wants, and looks like Brooke is going to take full advantage of that." Claire lifted her wine glass in the direction of the tables.

The knot in Izzy's stomach tightened as she saw Brian was no longer with Carol and Frank. Brooke was standing next to him as they talked with Marty and his wife, Kristen. At first glance, it appeared like a group of friends simply talking to each other. However, Izzy caught the way Brooke would rub Brian's arm when she spoke to him. Izzy finished her wine in one gulp.

"I need another drink," she said as she headed to the bar, Claire following behind her.

Another glass of wine in hand, Izzy was thankful that Claire had remained quiet. She needed time to process this. Unfortunately for her, she wouldn't get that time as Barb and Charlie came over to chat with them, followed closely by Tim and his wife, Sophie. It wasn't long before Greg joined them, along with Liza. The group's conversation turned loud and was filled with laughter as Barb told stories of Charlie's most recent mishaps. Tim joined in with a few colorful stories of some of the most recent police calls.

Izzy was enjoying herself. It was true, she thought, that laughter was the best medicine. Eventually, Tim and Sophie went to get food and sit at a table. Barb and Charlie weren't far behind. The rest picked out a table, set their things down and went to get their own dinner.

Plate in hand, Izzy was trying to decide between the ham and the broiled flounder when she heard Brian's voice. "Hey, Izzy." It was a simple greeting but it startled her.

Hoping it didn't show, she smiled at him. "Hi, Brian."

"You look nice tonight."

Izzy felt her smile broaden and her cheeks flush. "Thank you."

Brian hesitated a moment and then, "Look, Iz, do you think —"

"There you are!" Brooke exclaimed, rushing up to them. "I've been looking for you. We're going to sit with Tim and Sophie, is that okay?" Brooke turned and gave Izzy a smile. "Hi, Izzy."

Izzy mustered a smile. "Hi, Brooke." Looking at Brian she said, "Don't let me keep you." She stabbed some ham, put it on her plate and walked to her table. The knot in her stomach was replaced by something akin to nausea.

Her ears were buzzing and she could barely hear the conversation throughout dinner. She tried to follow it, nodding occasionally, but she couldn't get past the buzzing or the thought of Brian with Brooke. She had to keep reminding herself that he was free to associate with whoever he wanted, she had no right to be angry, upset or anything else.

What came next, what she did hear loud and clear, Izzy was in no way prepared for.

Tim's voice boomed over the buzzing and the chatter of the room, "I can't believe this! Ethan Kennedy!"

Izzy dropped her fork. She looked up at Claire. Claire had been about to take a sip of water, her glass stopped mid-way to her mouth. Claire eyes went from the back corner of the room over to Izzy. Izzy heard Greg mutter something and she felt Liza's hand on her arm.

Turning slowly, her heart began to beat faster. There he was. Ethan. Snowflakes were sprinkled in his hair, his coat still on. He looked exactly the same as he had three years ago. Izzy saw Tim point in her direction. She saw Ethan's face break into a wide smile as he began to walk toward her.

As Ethan came closer, Izzy noticed he did not look exactly the same. His dark hair was longer and he was sporting the start of a beard. Time seemed to speed up yet stand still at the same time. She took in details. He looked paler, his brown eyes didn't seem to have that sparkle they once did. She saw he still walked in that same self-assured, confident way he had.

Izzy felt herself getting up from the table. Ethan greeted her without words. He drew her into a hug and squeezed her tightly. She felt as if she had gone into auto-pilot. Returning the hug, she breathed in his scent. It was different. Where once he smelled of pine and cedar, he now smelled of a cologne she couldn't identify. His arms around her felt familiar, yet she couldn't relax into them like she once had.

Moving back a bit, without releasing her from the hug, Ethan gave her a light kiss and then gently stroked her hair. "It's good to see you, Isabella," he said with a tilt of his head and a small smile.

"Ethan," Izzy's voice was almost a whisper, "what are you doing here?"

Ethan chuckled softly. "Isn't it obvious? I came here for you, silly."

"It's been a long time," Greg interrupted them. "How have you been, Ethan?"

Releasing Izzy, Ethan turned to the table and greeted Greg, Claire and Liza. Replying to Greg, Ethan said, "I've been pretty good, Greg. I can't complain at all." Wrapping an arm around Izzy, he continued, "I can't wait for this girl to come to the city and see it for herself. She's going to love the city."

Izzy saw Claire pick up her wine and look back at Ethan. She couldn't tell what Claire was thinking. There was too much noise in Izzy's head for her to think clearly. She tried to clear her mind but everything seemed too surreal and out of focus. It felt like someone else was inhabiting her body and she was only a spectator. Then she seemed to zero in on something.

"Ethan, I never called you back. I never told you I was going to New York."

"I know, honey. That's why I'm here. I was reminded. . .it hit me. . . that you love this kind of sappy thing. I mean, how romantic can it get? There's snow outside, it's the holiday season, and I drove up here to sweep you off your feet and take you back to New York with me." Ethan drew her closer to him.

At that moment, Tim, Marty and a few other friends came up to surround Ethan and welcome him to the party. Ethan dropped his arm away from Izzy and turned to them, told them how great it was to see everyone again and delved into conversation. Izzy took the moment to pick up her wine and take a sip.

Catching Claire's eye, Izzy saw her friend wasn't happy with this development. Izzy raised her shoulders and gave her a look she hoped conveyed that she wasn't expecting this and had no clue how to handle it. Claire got up and came around the table to her.

"Are you okay?" Claire asked.

"I don't know," Izzy replied honestly. "I didn't know he was coming. I can't think straight." She paused for a moment. "I feel blocked, if that makes sense. I can't seem to feel anything and my mind can't focus. It feels like an out-of-body experience."

Claire nodded. "Well," she said, "he did drive up here knowing a snowstorm is supposed to be coming. You can give him points for that, I guess, but I will say – is it really a romantic gesture if you have to advertise that it is? It's more like a self-centered grand entrance if you ask me."

"Don't," Izzy said quietly. "Please."

"Okay, fine. But, Izzy," Claire pulled her so they were standing face to face, Claire's hands on her upper arms, "you have to decide. I know you weren't expecting this, but you have to decide. The longer Brian sees you with Ethan, the farther away he'll get. If you want to go with Ethan, that's fine. But if you don't, you need to decide that and tell Ethan."

Izzy nodded. Then she let out a short breath. "Ethan sounds like he's already decided that for me, but this isn't the place for me to talk to him. There are too many people, and I need to find out what he really wants. I mean, Claire, I used to pray he'd come back. He's here now."

Not responding at first, Claire gave Izzy's arms a rub before dropping her hands away. "I know you did." Claire paused and gave her head a slight shake. "I just wish you'd see it."

"See what?" Izzy asked.

Claire looked at her friend with an expression Izzy couldn't discern. Was it concern? Sympathy? Resignation? Izzy didn't know. When Claire spoke again, her voice was quiet, "I can't make you see it, Izzy. I tried. I can tell you but you'll deny it."

Before Izzy could respond, Ethan turned around and pulled her to him again. She found herself in the circle of guys that had come over to welcome Ethan back. Giving Tim a small smile, she tried to pick up the thread of conversation.

"This is great," Marty said. "I can't believe you showed up. We'll have to go to Misty's and do some shots, just like we used to."

Tim laughed. "I don't know if I can do as many as I used to, but I'll sure try!"

"Maybe," Ethan said, "but I'm not sure how long I'm going to be here." He turned to Izzy. "I mean, I came back for this girl." He kissed the side of her head.

Tim shook his head, "Yeah, okay. We got it. Make an entrance, get the girl, and leave. I don't know if you're gonna be able to leave, though. I told you the other day a storm is coming. The snow has already started. It'll get heavier later. Driving back won't be an option."

Izzy felt Ethan shrug. "Then I'll get snowed in with my beautiful girl here."

Her head swimming, Izzy tried to focus on Ethan. She took in his profile as he continued talking to the guys. For a moment, she saw the Ethan of three years ago; clean shaven, shorter hair and that easy laugh. Memories came back to her. She remembered how much she had loved him, the mornings spent by the sea, the walks they took, and the talks they had.

There was something else, though. She felt something was trying to break through. Something that seemed separate from Ethan was in the back of her mind and was trying to come forward. She tried to block out the noise. It was almost there when Ethan shook her from her thoughts.

He pulled her into another hug and whispered in her ear, "What do you say we get out of here. I'm done doing the reunion with the town thing. The only reunion I want is with you."

Over Ethan's shoulder, she saw Brian get up from his table, grab his coat and walk to the doorway. He took a look back at Izzy. They held eyes for only a second before he walked through the doorway. She could only assume he was leaving. Brooke followed a second behind him, but Izzy noticed she hadn't taken her coat with her. Her head began to throb as images of both Brian and Ethan floated through her mind. Whatever was in the back of her mind was banging against the memories. The buzzing in

172

her ears returned. Izzy swayed a little as she began to feel light-headed.

Pulling back from Ethan, she looked him in the eyes. More memories of their time together flooded through her, but the banging continued. "Excuse me, Ethan," she said hurriedly. "I need to use the ladies room."

Practically running to the ladies room, she threw the door open and went to the line of sinks. She steadied herself against them and took deep breaths. Whatever her mind wanted her to remember was about to come out and she wasn't sure she was ready for it.

If He Comes Back

THIRTEEN

"Izzy! Are you okay?"

Izzy turned to see Claire coming through the door. She shook her head, turned the water on, and splashed some cold water on her cheeks. Turning to Claire, she felt the tears in her eyes start to burn.

"I don't know what's happening, Claire. This isn't normal. I can't focus and the thoughts in my head are loud."

"Okay, okay," Claire said soothingly, "Take a seat." Claire guided her to the loveseat in the corner then went back to the sink to grab some paper towels and handed them to Izzy.

Izzy took the towels and patted her face as Claire sat down beside her and wrapped an arm around her. "I don't know what it is. I was fine, then I started to hear this buzzing in my ears. It got worse when Ethan showed up. The last few minutes, I don't know. It's like my brain is trying to tell me something. I feel like I'm losing my mind."

The tears began to fall. Claire held onto her and let Izzy release them, remaining silent. After a few minutes, the sobs had stopped and

Izzy was taking deep breaths. Using a paper towel to wipe the tears away, Izzy sat upright again. She used the other towel to blow her nose. Clearing her throat, she waited until she could speak without her voice cracking.

"A few months ago, everything was fine. I was fine. Life was pretty good. Then Brian came back and it was good. It really was. Then Ethan texted. . .and then everything got strange." Izzy paused for a moment, sniffling. "Brian was wonderful. I was really happy. I was beginning to think. . .I don't know what I was beginning to think. I spent three years wishing Ethan would come back to me and he has. He's here. It's what I wanted now I don't know. My mind won't stop. I feel like I'm literally falling apart."

"I'm not a therapist, Izzy. I'm not sure how to get you through this. I'm just going to ask you a few questions and let's see if we can get to why you're having this reaction."

Izzy nodded, "Okay."

Claire took Izzy's hand. "You said you were happy with Brian. I know you were, I saw it. You hadn't looked like that in a long time. Were you falling in love with him again?"

Taking a moment, Izzy nodded, "Yes. I think I was." Tears began to fill her eyes again.

"I want you to think before answering this. If you were falling in love with Brian, why did Ethan's text have that effect on you?"

"I wasn't expecting it. I mean it came out of nowhere and he said he really missed me. I guess because I had been waiting for a long time to hear it."

"Okay, but you still had Brian. You were happy. You were falling in love. What made you decide to take Ethan up on his offer if you were happy with Brian?"

Not answering right away, Izzy looked down, thinking about how she was feeling when she made the decision. She looked back at Claire. "I think because I wanted Ethan to come back for so long I felt I owed it to myself to. . . I don't know." She stopped.

"Okay," Claire said calmly, "but what about your feelings for Brian? How did they compare to what you built up in your mind with Ethan?"

Izzy tilted her head at Claire. "Built up in my mind?"

"He's been gone for three years, Izzy. I know you said you don't want to hear this again but don't you think that over time you began to think things with Ethan were better than what they actually were?"

"I know you said I was romanticizing it. I don't know." Izzy shook her head and was about to deny it, but then she remembered all the times she would sit with Jasper at night and imagine what it would be like to have Ethan there beside her. Maybe she had been. She closed her eyes and inhaled. "What does that matter, though? He's here now. He actually did come back."

"He didn't come back, Izzy," Claire replied. "He's here to take you to New York. He didn't come back to stay here. Brian did. Ethan won't."

"Yeah, well," Izzy snorted, "Ethan wasn't the only one who left this town. Brian did, too, you know. It's not like everybody stays."

"What makes you think Brian won't?" Claire prodded.

Izzy almost shouted, "Because everybody leaves! Everyone I love leaves. My parents left, Brian left, Ethan left. I'm surprised you haven't left, too." She exhaled sharply.

Gently, Claire took both of Izzy's hands and looked her in the eyes. "And that's what you've been afraid of."

"*What?*" Izzy shook her head and took her hands out from Claire's. "I'm tired of people telling me I'm afraid. Liza said something, too. I'm not afraid, I was stating facts." Suddenly a sentence Brian had said to her when he first came back to town went through her mind. She turned back to Claire. "Tell me what you're seeing that I can't."

"You said it yourself. You think everyone you love leaves you. I think it scared you when you realized you were falling in love with Brian again. I think on some level you thought –"

"That he was going to leave again." Izzy finished the sentence. She let the thought sink into her mind. Remembering the night she told Brian about Ethan, she recalled throwing the fact that he had once left back at him. She also remembered he didn't finish what he had started saying. He reminded her they had come to the decision to end their previous relationship mutually and that it was not the same thing as what happened with Ethan, but there had been something else he was going to say and didn't.

A long-forgotten memory burst through. Brian had come home for a couple weeks between his junior and senior year of college. He came to her parent's house and took her for a walk. The memory was so vivid now, she couldn't believe she hadn't remembered it.

Standing on the corner by the factory, he'd asked her if she wanted to get back together. Remembering her answer as if she had uttered the words only yesterday, her hand went to her mouth. She had told him she loved him but that if he left her once, he might leave her again and she couldn't put her heart through that. He told her he hadn't left her, he went to college. She told him they'd broken up *because* he'd left for college and the long-distance thing hadn't worked. She remembered Brian telling her that didn't make sense, that he would come back after graduation and they would do all the things they had talked about.

He didn't know her parents had already announced they were moving to Arizona at the end of that year. She remembered feeling as if her life was being upended. She began counting off the names of people they had known that had left town and then she added his name to the end of the list. The last thing she remembered from that conversation was telling him that once people left, they didn't seem to come back.

Izzy sat with the memory and let it sink in. She thought of what Claire had noticed. She thought about her parents leaving, she thought about when Brian had left and, lastly, when Ethan left. Looking at Claire, she said. "I think I may have abandonment issues."

"You think?" Claire smiled at her. "Not everyone leaves, Izzy. What you also don't seem to get is this; just because someone might leave town, it doesn't mean they stop loving you. You know that. You still hear from people that left, and they make sure to see you when they come back and visit."

Izzy nodded, but didn't reply. She laid her head on Claire's shoulder and let the tears come again. "It was so hard after my parents left," Izzy sniffled. "When I told them I didn't want to go to Arizona, they said that was okay. I could go with them if I wanted, I could stay if I wanted, but . . ."

"But instead of feeling like they respected your decision and were treating you like an adult who could handle being on her own, you thought they didn't care."

"That's true," Izzy said through the tears. "I did feel that way."

"It wasn't you they wanted to get away from, honey. It was the horrible winters." Claire began to laugh. "Your dad hated winter the last few years he was here. I can still hear him bitching about the cold, the snow, the shoveling, the plows."

Izzy let out a chuckle, "So can I." She sat up and wiped her eyes. "He actually paid Brian to do all our shoveling. He said if he had to lift one more shovel he was going to jump in the lake. I remember saying he could jump in the lake if he really wanted to, but a snow blower would be a better answer. Unless, of course, he was dead set on taking a swan dive into the lake." Izzy chuckled. "He didn't like that."

Izzy was silent for a moment and then continued. "After Brian left for his senior year, I was kind of hoping he would come back to stay like he said he would. When he didn't, I thought, well there's another one, even though I was the one that nixed getting back together. Then Ethan left and I guess that was the nail in the coffin."

The tears began to fall again and she buried her head against Claire's shoulder as Claire once again held her friend. "No one loved me enough to stay with me," Izzy said through the tears.

Claire waited until the tears subsided and then lifted Izzy off her shoulder. She put her hands on the sides of Izzy head. "You're wrong. Your parents love you more than life itself, they only wanted to get away from this climate. They're happy where they are and they can't wait until you visit every year. I grew up with you, remember? There is no doubt about how much they love you.

"As for Brian, he adored you. He wanted to get back together. His timing was just really off and, yeah, you kind of gave him permission - so to speak - not to come back. But just think about it, Izzy. If Brian wasn't planning on staying in Willow's End now, he wouldn't have bought his parents house and he certainly never would have thought about buying the factory. And I think we both know why he wants the factory."

Izzy admitted that was true. She looked at Claire. "I really do think I was falling in love again and he definitely is trying to make things permanent." She paused for a few moments. "I'm still back where I started, though," she said. "What am I going to do? Ethan's out there. He wants me to see what he's done in New York. He called me his girl again. I know things weren't perfect, Claire. I know I may have romanticized it over the years, but I did love him."

"I know. I think what you need to do is follow your heart. You will let one of them down, you can't avoid that. But, Izzy, you need to listen to your heart. I will be here to support whatever decision you make, I promise." Claire hugged her tightly.

"Thank you," Izzy whispered, then sat back. "I think I need to be alone for a bit. I need to get myself together before I go back out there."

"I'll leave you to your thoughts," Claire said as she stood up, "just promise me that you will decide what is best for *you*, what's going to make *you* happy."

"I promise," Izzy answered.

Left alone, Izzy exhaled and leaned back. She took in Claire's words and a sense of calm came over her. Her parents did love her, she knew that. She decided that she would call them the next day and ask them if they had been confident she could handle living on her own. She knew they would say yes because, after all, she had succeeded in doing it. She smiled to herself as she realized she had never acknowledged or given herself credit for the work she did to succeed on her own.

Closing her eyes, a thousand images went through her mind. Bits and pieces of conversations with the friends who had left and only come back to visit. She realized they, too, not only hadn't forgotten her but still considered her a good friend.

Then thoughts of moments with both Brian and Ethan reverberated in her head. So many of them made her smile, others made her think. She began to feel torn between the past and the present, a tangle of emotions and conflicting desires.

Izzy knew she had to confront her true feelings head-on and put aside any doubts or fears that she had been harboring. She slowed her breathing and let her mind wander through the memories, through the conversations she'd had with both of them and through the feelings she had for them. She began sorting out what was real from what was imagined.

She realized the buzzing in her head had subsided and the tangled mess in her mind was beginning to unravel. She could think more clearly, and she could see things more clearly as the memories, images and words passed through.

As her emotions and her heart began to take over from the logical thought process, she knew. Truth be told, she knew before her heart took over, it just couldn't wait much longer. Without warning, a clear vision of what she wanted and a plan to get there had formed in her head. A sense of purpose washed over her. She knew exactly what she wanted to do, and was prepared to make it happen.

Feeling a weight had been lifted from her, she got up, made her way out of the bathroom and back to the table. She looked around but didn't see Ethan. Looking at Claire, she asked, "Where did Ethan go?"

Claire shrugged and Greg answered, "He went with Frank to see the new pool table they got in what they now call the game room."

Looking back at Claire, Izzy smiled. "I know what I'm going to do. I just need some help."

Standing up, Claire said, "You got it. What do you want me to do?"

After quickly relaying her plan to Claire, Izzy grabbed her coat and left the inn. There were two places she needed to stop before she could set it up exactly the way she had seen it in her vision. Running through the snow, she felt rejuvenated. This had to work, she thought. It just had to.

FOURTEEN

Lighting the last candle, Izzy looked around. The fairy lights she had hurriedly hung twinkled, the candles gave the room a warm glow, and the blanket in the middle of the floor looked inviting in the candlelight. If she had more time, she could have made it look more magical, but this would do. She had sent the text after she hung the lights. She estimated she only had a minute or two left. Looking around, she decided it looked beautiful despite the limited time. With nothing else left to do, Izzy took a seat and waited, her heart nearly beating out of her chest.

Fifteen minutes later, when Izzy had begun to think it wouldn't work and he wasn't coming, she heard the door downstairs open and close. Closing her eyes, she bit her lip and smiled. She heard slow footsteps coming up the steps and then across the floor, stopping right before they reached her.

"It was always you," Izzy said, not turning around. "It was true then and it's true now." Standing up, she took a deep breath before turning to face him. "It was always you."

Brian was standing still, arms at his side, regarding Izzy with a calm expression. His eyes shifted, taking in the candles and the lights. The light from the candles gave both the walls of the factory and Izzy a warm and inviting glow. His gaze returned to Izzy.

"What made you realize it?" He finally asked.

"I think I always knew it. I was too blind to see it." Izzy paused, twisting the ring on her little finger. "I was afraid," she continued, her voice cracking slightly. "I couldn't see it. Then I remembered something you said about listening to your friends because they see things that you can't." She let out a little laugh. "It's true. Claire didn't exactly tell me what she saw, she kind of led me there and waited until I figured it out."

"What were you afraid of, Izzy?"

Izzy looked down. She was almost afraid of putting a voice to it. "That you would leave again." She looked up again. "I had a belief, I guess, that everyone leaves. That no one ever loved me enough to stay. I think that's why I kind of went off the rails."

Brian closed the distance between them. "You're wrong." Izzy nodded. "You're wrong," Brian said again.

"I know," Izzy answered. "Claire helped me see that, but I think it's going to take some time before I start to actually believe it."

"Izzy, I'm not going anywhere."

Looking up and meeting his eyes, Izzy replied. "That's what I'm hoping."

"That's what's true," Brian said. "And Ethan?"

Sighing, Izzy put her hands up to her face for a second and then brought them back down. "I'm not going to lie, I did love him. What I realized tonight was that, even though I loved him, or believed I did, and said I wanted to marry him, on some level I knew it wasn't going to last. I think there was a part of me that knew it would have ended, even if he had stayed here. There's some kind of name for that, but I don't know what it is."

"I know what you mean. Self-fulfilling prophecy, maybe? Or maybe like when women only date married men - it's because they know it's not going to go anywhere."

"Yeah, kind of, I guess. Then after he left, I just built this whole thing up in my head to avoid getting involved with anyone. It was easier to live with memories and an active imagination than admit you're afraid of people leaving because your parents moved away and then a long time ago you let the right one slip away from you."

She saw a small smile form on Brian's face, but then he said. "Ethan came back for you."

"But I'm not going anywhere." Izzy saw Brian smile again, though it was a closed-lip smile, not the broad one she desperately wanted to see. "I'm so sorry, Brian. I never wanted to hurt you. I know that sounds so cliché, but it's true. I was scared and didn't realize it. I used Ethan as an excuse. I didn't know that's what I was doing until tonight. Everything finally became clear to me tonight. I hope. . .I hope. . ." She stopped.

"You hope what, Izzy?" Brian asked, his voice deep and calm.

"I hope it's not too late. I hope I didn't mess this up beyond repair. I hope we can start again. I hope you don't hate me." She inhaled, held it for a moment and then exhaled slowly.

Brian didn't reply. He moved a little closer, his head tilted to the side. Izzy felt her heart race. She wanted to wrap her arms around him, she wanted to kiss him. Instead, she said the words she hadn't said to him for ten years.

"I love you, Brian."

His hands came up and he held both sides of her head as he leaned in and kissed her. Izzy's arms went around him, hands resting on his back. Izzy felt a fire within her she hadn't felt for so long. Her hands slid up his back and she dug in as they went back down. Brian's hands went to her shoulders and then slid down to her waist, one hand went behind her and pressed her closer to him.

His lips went down to her neck and then to her ear lobe. He whispered in her ear, "I love you, too, Isabella Maria Rossi."

Moving his head back, he looked her in the eyes. "It's always been you, Iz. I never stopped loving you." He kissed her again. "I thought you had moved on, so that's what I did."

Izzy kissed him. "I was young." Another kiss. "And stupid." She kissed him again. "I should never have let you go that day on the corner."

Brian simultaneously kissed her and picked her up. Izzy wrapped her legs around him, her hands going through his hair. He moved to the middle of the room, carefully knelt down and laid her on the blanket. She reached up and unbuttoned his shirt. Reaching inside she grazed her nails down his chest. Brian slid the straps of her dress down until she pulled her arms through them. He reached underneath her and unclasped her bra. Taking it off, she threw it to the side. He bent his head down and kissed her neck, then moved his head and lightly kissed the valley between her breasts.

Unable to hold back any longer, they tore the rest of their clothes off and paused for only a moment. Breathing heavily, naked, limbs entwined, they looked deeply into each other's eyes. Izzy had never felt so in love before. She saw that same feeling reflected in Brian's eyes and when he entered her she let out a moan so deep she surprised herself. Within seconds they were in the perfect rhythm, never breaking their eye contact. When they climaxed, Izzy grasped Brian's hair as he pressed his head against her shoulder and released the pent up emotions he had held onto for nearly ten years.

Wrapped in the blanket, holding each other, Brian was stroking Izzy's hair. Her eyes closed, Izzy only wanted to revel in the afterglow. She wanted to stay this way for as long as she could.

"Hey," Brian said softly, "how'd you get in here, anyway? And why is it warm in here?"

Opening her eyes, Izzy moved and propped herself up on her elbow. "I was waiting for you to ask me that." She smiled. "I asked Claire to have Marty open the door and turn the heat up."

"When did you plan this?" Brian sat up and looked down at her. "You couldn't have planned this before the party."

"No," she said. "The moment it hit me, I had a vision." She waved her hand around the room. "This vision. Although, it would have been better if I'd had more time. I asked Claire to help me. She talked to Marty, got the candles from Carol for me and brought them here. I ran home to get the lights and this blanket. It had to be this blanket."

Brian looked at the blanket, a bit confused. Then his expression changed to surprise. "Are you kidding me? Is this? No, it can't be!"

"It is. The blanket we took to Winding Lake the first time we made love." Izzy smiled. "I held onto it. I just kept it folded in the back of the closet, never really sure why. Now I know why." She shrugged. "It was always you."

"You were pretty sure of yourself if you ran home to get this blanket."

"I wasn't sure," Izzy replied. "I was hoping." Then she remembered something. "Oh my God, I can't believe I forgot! Home wasn't the only place I stopped." She rolled over and pulled her dress over her head.

Getting up, she held out her hand to Brian. Wrapping himself in the blanket, he took Izzy's hand and stood up.

"Where are we going?" Brian asked. "I'm not sure I can take any more surprises tonight. First, you break into the factory, then you confess your undying love before practically throwing yourself at me. What else can you possibly do?"

Izzy raised her eyebrows. "First of all, I didn't break in. I had accomplices. Second, it's going to be *your* factory anyway. Third, I'm not the only one who confessed their love and last — are you complaining?"

"Not - at - all," Brian said and smiled. Izzy's heart leaped as she saw that broad smile she loved. The one that reached his eyes and lit up his entire face.

"Good," Izzy said as she picked up a candle and led Brian to the corner of the room. "This might be a bit presumptuous of me, but I think you'll understand."

Lifting the candle to illuminate the wall, Izzy held her breath. There, on the wall, on the second story of the old shoe factory, where they had once planned to have a gallery, was Izzy's painting of Winding Lake. She looked over at Brian. He was looking at the painting, a smile crept over his face, and it could have been the candlelight but she thought she saw his eyes water.

"It's perfect. That painting is perfect. That painting is us," Brian said and leaned over to kiss her. Looking back at it, he was silent for a minute before he made the observation. "You know, you weren't supposed to know about me buying the building. I don't want to know who let it slip. I was hoping we could mold it into our dream. Then you said you were thinking about New York–"

"No," Izzy cut him off. "New York was Ethan's dream." She turned to Brian and put a hand on his cheek. "This. This right here. This is *my* dream."

"No."

Izzy dropped her hand. "No?"

"It's not *your* dream, Izzy. It's *our* dream," Brian said, "and we're going to make it come true. I wanted to surprise you. I wanted to give you a romantic moment that would rival any movie you ever saw. He paused and smiled at her, putting his hand on her cheek. "Turns out you gave me one."

"You gave me one the moment I saw you standing on my porch." Izzy covered his hand with her own.

Outside, the snow storm began in earnest, but neither one of them cared.

FIFTEEN

"Make way for the unruly boy!" Izzy greeted Claire and Greg as Jasper made his way into their house.

"Which one? Jasper or Brian?" Claire asked with a laugh.

"Both of us," Brian answered as he handed Claire the dessert and Greg the bottle of whiskey they brought.

"Now that's what I like," Greg said as he looked at the bottle.

"Well, then, let's open it," Brian said as Greg walked him into the kitchen.

Claire took Izzy's coat and hung it in the closet. Turning back to Izzy, Claire gave her a big smile. "You look so radiant, Izzy. I guess that's what good sex'll do for you."

"Stop it!" Izzy laughed, then lowered her voice. "But I gotta say, he's learned a lot over the last ten years. Let me tell you, if you hadn't invited us to dinner, we'd still be in bed." Taking her voice back to normal volume, she continued, "It's so much more than that, though. I can't even describe it. It's like the world has colors again. All I know is if I could still do cartwheels, I would."

"There she is," Claire held up her hands. "It's so nice to have the old Izzy back. I've missed her so much!" She gave Izzy's shoulders a squeeze.

"Wow. Was I really that bad the last few years?" Izzy asked, a bit incredulous.

Claire tilted her head from side to side "No, not bad, per se, but whether you want to admit it or not, Ethan really dampened your spirit, then when he left, it was nearly extinguished. You weren't bad, just . . ." Claire couldn't seem to find the right words.

"Not who I used to be," Izzy offered.

"Exactly," Claire said. "Listen, I've barely had a chance to talk to you since the party. Yeah, we talked on the phone, but not for long. Everything got so hectic, as it normally does this time of year and, apparently, when you've had free time, you've spent it in bed."

"Not true," Izzy said, holding up a finger. "I've been at the store, we've walked Jasper, we've been to Misty's - and I did manage to get the shopping done and the house cleaned."

"Yeah, in-between," Claire joked. "Seriously, though, tell me what happened in that bathroom after I left. I almost came back because I was worried, but then, suddenly, you come out and you have this plan. I mean, yeah, you and Brian got back together and we've talked since, but you never said what happened in there."

Izzy smiled and tried to find the words to describe it to Claire. "I don't know. It was definitely an epiphany. Once I realized what I was afraid of – you know, that thing everyone saw except me - my mind seemed to quiet down. I no longer heard all the noise. I just closed my eyes and all these things went through my mind. Then suddenly, it just clicked. It all became clear. Things wouldn't have worked with Ethan, even if he hadn't left. I know that now. I really thought I wanted to marry him, but the truth is he was a replacement. Or that's what my therapist says, a replacement that I knew wouldn't last.

"It was always Brian. Claire, look at the things I did. After Ethan left, I never went out to the rocks to see the sunrise. If I wanted to paint the sunrise, I went down toward the pier. On the I spent a lot of time at Winding Lake. I mfort there. And when I did did I do without even d in one the trees that had one where Brian and I had carved our initials. Everything pointed to Brian. Always. Even the fact that I held onto our blanket."

"Blanket?" Claire asked.

Izzy shook her head. "Don't ask. I'll never hear the end of it if you do."

"Now I have to know," Claire said.

"No, you don't. Anyway, there were other things I remember, too. I always thought Ethan and I were on the same page, but we really weren't. He'd make these decisions and would act as if we'd made them together. He even did that at the party. The more I look back on it…"

"The more he seems like an asshole?" Claire asked with an eyebrow raised. "Everyone saw it, Izzy. He came in and acted like you'd already agreed to pick up and move to New York after barely talking to you for months. I almost spit out my drink when he called you his girl. I know you thought it was endearing at the time, when we talked in the bathroom, but you hadn't even told him you were going to visit and he already had you guys back together, acting like you wanted that, too."

Izzy hid her face in her hands, then sh peeked out at Claire between her fingers.

more she had reflected on her relationship with Ethan the more she realized Claire had been right. She had morphed it into this perfect, loving relationship in her mind when the reality was that Ethan had always called the shots and, as Claire had hinted at, she had lost herself.

"You know what? Next time just hit me over the head with a brick."

"There won't be a next time," Claire said. "You and Brian are it. Oh! And in case you didn't know, Tim was keeping in touch with Ethan. It was Tim that let Ethan know about Brian. I don't think Tim realized what he was doing. I believe he honestly thought it was just friends keeping in touch."

"I know," Izzy said. "I realized that, too, when I was in the bathroom. Tim said he'd told Ethan about the storm. I didn't pick up on it when he said it, but as I was thinking about things it clicked. I'm pretty sure Tim found out about the factory. I think that's why Ethan drove up to make his grand entrance.

"You and Greg were right. Ethan wouldn't have gotten back in touch with me if I hadn't been seeing Brian. He came back to claim his property. Classic case of not wanting someone, but not wanting anyone else to have them, either."

"He didn't deserve you then and certainly doesn't deserve you now."

Izzy softened. "I hope he finds whatever dream he's chasing in New York. I really do. Everyone deserves to be happy. For him, I hope he finds it in New York. Or Los Angeles. Or Seattle. Wherever, as long as it's not here."

Claire chuckled and Izzy scrunched up her face. "That wasn't fair. I do wish him well. Honestly. That reminds me, though. I never asked - what happened to him after I left the party? He seemed to vanish."

"Well," Claire started, "I was busy talking to Marty and getting the candles from Carol when Ethan came back to the hall. He asked Greg where you were and Greg told him you'd gone after Brian and he should leave you alone. He started to argue, but Greg told him Brian made you happier than he'd ever seen you and if Ethan cared about you at all, he'd leave."

Izzy's eyes widened. "Wow. Remind me to thank Greg." She fell silent for a moment. "And Brooke?"

"That was really nothing more than wishful thinking on Brooke's part. I honestly feel empathy for her, though. She hasn't had it easy and she saw an opportunity."

It was a true statement. Brooke's life hadn't been easy since her husband died. Izzy couldn't blame her for making a play for Brian. Under the same circumstances, she would have done the same. She hoped that one day Brooke would find the kind of love she had.

After dinner, gathered around the fireplace in the living room, talk of the highway dominated the conversation. Izzy reiterated her stance of not wanting the town to become too commercialized. Greg agreed, though added that the extra tourism would definitely give the town a boost. Claire gave her own ideas, saying the extra money coming in would help give the town a facelift. She envisioned old-fashioned street lights on the main street and power washing the old brick buildings to give them a well-kept look.

"Speaking of old brick buildings," Greg said, "let's talk about the factory, Brian. Hotel? Apartments? Air BnB?"

"Definitely not an Air BnB," Brian answered. "Iz and I have been talking it over and we're going to stick to our original plan, for the most part."

"What's staying and what are you changing?" Claire asked.

Izzy answered, "We're sticking to the original plan with the first and second floors. I'll be moving the bookstore to the second floor. It's the third and the fourth floor we're debating on. We're not sure if we want to go with apartments or hotel rooms, given the highway situation."

"Go with apartments," Greg said. "We may need a hotel or another inn, but let someone else build that on the edge of town. Keep that building for people that live here. That's my two cents."

"Hold on," Claire said. "So, the first floor restaurant - are you going to be the chef, Brian?"

"Maybe. Not sure I want to give up my IT business just yet," Brian answered. "I certainly want to set the menu. It will definitely have French cuisine." He turned to Izzy. "Just like we planned."

Claire had another question. "Wasn't the second floor supposed to be a gallery?"

Brian gave Izzy a smile before answering Claire. "That's the part she left out when she told you she's moving the bookstore. I've finally convinced her to sell some of her paintings. So, in a sense, there will be a small gallery."

Izzy blushed as Greg and Claire gushed over the fact she finally agreed to sell her work.

She had started a new painting in the previous days. It was the factory in its heyday, before it lost its competitive edge. That one would not be for sale. She wanted it hung in the restaurant as a reminder of days gone by.

She'd actually finished a painting that Brian was unaware of. It was a portrait of them, leaning against their willow tree at Winding Lake, complete with their carved initials above them. It was wrapped and sitting behind the Christmas tree at her house, waiting for Christmas Day. Though, it didn't feel like *her* house anymore. Brian had decided to sell his father's house and he moved into hers. They were in the process of making it their home.

Home. Brian had come home, to the place where he had been the happiest. The place where he found happiness again, a place filled with love. Together, Izzy and Brian would make their dream come true. For Izzy, she realized that even though she had never left Willow's End, with Brian she knew her heart had finally come home.

If He Comes Back

Kate Browning lives in Georgia with her husband, dog and two cats. You can contact her via email at: kate.browning@mjcmediapa.com

ACKNOWLEDGEMENTS

I'd like to thank everyone at MJC Media for their encouragement and support. Without it, I'd be lost. I would also like to thank my husband and my daughter, who put up with me being locked away to create my characters.

And to you, dear Reader, thank you for taking the time to read Izzy's story. I hope you enjoyed it!